Listen to Love

Val Portelli

Publishers: Quirky Unicorn Publications.
QuirkyUnicornBooks.Wordpress.com

If Music be the food of Love, Read on.

A collection of short stories with Love as their theme, but be prepared for some surprises.

Dementia, ghosts, murder, jealousy, second chances and even inanimate objects all find their place.

Before each story is a brief introduction, giving the background and inspiration.

Many were inspired by song titles, but the stories are as varied as Love itself.

About the author

Other books by Val Portelli (who also writes under the pen name Voinks) may be found on Amazon at:
www.amazon.co.uk/Val-Portelli/e/B01MVB8WNC
and
www.amazon.com/Voinks/e/B01MVB8WNC

The author is a prolific writer of short stories which can be found every week on her Facebook author page:
https://www.facebook.com/pg/Voinks.writer.author/posts

More information can be found on the publisher's web site at:
www.QuirkyUnicornBooks.Wordpress.com

on Goodreads:
www.goodreads.com/author/list/16843817.Val_Portelli

and her personal blog:
www.Voinks.Wordpress.com

For advance information and special offers, join her mailing list here:
https://voinks.wordpress.com/sign-up/

Acknowledgements:

Grateful things to my Beta Readers, in particular Paula Harmon for her work on the cover design, and general support.

Thanks also to the brilliant songwriters and singers who provided the inspiration for some of these stories.

Table of Contents

Making up for lost time.

Malta is a woman.

Message to Martha.

My Little friend.

Not Fade away.

Perfect Day.

Race with the Devil.

Save the last dance for me.

Take me with you.

Valentine's day.

Valentine's day chocolates.

When I need you.

You don't bring me flowers.

You don't own me.

A Tail of love and life.

Dedicated to Pacer and Mij.

There were four of us when I was young.
Like all siblings we fought and scrapped together
but being male and the strongest, if not the eldest, I
usually won.

Dad wasn't around to keep us in check, and
as I got bigger Mum stopped trying to control me.
The people who owned the house we lived in
sometimes tried to scold me, but after a while they
too gave up. At one stage there was even talk of
sending me away as they thought I was getting out
of control, but I kept it cool for a while and they
dropped the idea.

This was my neighbourhood, and I didn't
want to move somewhere else and have to start all
over again to prove myself. Here on the streets I
had respect. I knew them, and they knew me and
kept their distance. If some flash youngster wanted
to take me on, a look and a glare were usually
enough to make him back down.

1

Now and again they would push too far, and I would have to prove I still had what it takes. It wouldn't be long before they had to retreat and peace would reign until the next time a flash young male fancied his chances.

I will never forget the day my life changed.

There I was, doing nothing in particular, just enjoying the fresh air and thinking of heading home for dinner when Bam! She was standing on the corner, perfectly groomed with big brown eyes to die for. I tried to say "Hello" and for a moment she looked interested, but then the woman she was with turned and started walking off. After a brief backward glance, the female of my dreams followed her.

For the next few days I scoured the streets but couldn't catch a glimpse of her. I was so besotted that some of the district brothers started spreading stories I had gone soft, so for a while every day was conflict until I had put them back in their place.

Quite by chance I was wandering one day in a neighbourhood I didn't usually visit and there she was, looking out of the window of an enormous posh house, obviously owned by the sort of people I despised. Suddenly she saw me and her eyes lit up.

Sliding through the half open gate I went into the garden. A big fat woman, probably a servant, came rushing out brandishing a broom.

'We don't want your sort around here,' she screamed. 'Get back to where you belong before I call the authorities and have you locked up.'

On that occasion I beat a strategic retreat, but that didn't stop me going back time and time again, usually with the darkness of night as cover. Often my angel wasn't there, but the odd occasion when I managed to catch a glimpse of her was enough to keep me returning despite the dangers.

One perfect, unbelievable evening she was actually in the garden, and I had a few minutes to get to know her before someone inside the big house called her to say dinner was ready. After that, I made it a point to be there at the same time every evening; sometimes she was free to come and see me, sometimes there was no sign of her.

Then came the night I will remember all my life. I was on the point of giving up when she emerged from the front door and headed straight for the undergrowth where I was hiding. My animal instincts took off and we had carnal relations, right there and then in the bushes, under the cover of darkness.

All too soon the hated voices called and she had to leave me to return indoors, to what I had come to think of as her prison. I visited her often over the next nine weeks, seeing her blossom and bloom as her belly swelled with my offspring.

I suffered when I didn't see her, until that glorious day when she came out to see me, followed by three of the most beautiful pups you have ever seen. Well, with the mixture of my genes and hers, what would you expect?

I'm not a pedigree like her, so I will never get to know my offspring. I hope they haven't been drowned or put down, and pray they have found a loving home somewhere. Although I never saw my lovely bitch again, I will always remember her.

I'm at the vets now, the injection is poised. In human years I'm probably well into my 90s, but I've had a good life and I'm not afraid to leave it. I hope one of my pups survived to be loved for themselves by a human family who think mongrels are worth more than pedigrees.

Slipping away now, hope God likes Dogs.

Final woof.

American Trilogy.

Elvis Presley released this wonderful song in 1972, but it was a tribute artist, Redent Falzon, who inspired me to write this story after listening to his version.

'Come on then, Kathy, tell us all about this new man in your life.'

'Yes, we want to know all the gory details. Where did you meet him?'

'His name's Jake. He's American. I met him at the gym and he's drop-dead gorgeous.'

'It's not like you to chat up strangers, Kath. How did you get talking?'

'I was on my way out, all hot and sweaty and looking like something the cat dragged in when I noticed him. I was so busy ogling I tripped over my own feet, ended up flat on the floor, and he came over to check I was alright. He's really sweet and caring. What about you, Pam? I heard you have a new fella as well.'

'Yeah, he's such a hoot. I haven't stopped laughing since we met. Oh, and he's American too. What a coincidence.'

'You always did go for guys with a sense of humour, Pam. Looks aren't everything. What's his name?'

'John. And he's a hunk. We met at the pool and he rocks those speedos. Whew, I'm getting hot just thinking about it. What about you, Sue. Any news on the man front?'

'No, I'm still billy no mates- apart from you two, of course. Anyway, I've got to get back to work. See you tomorrow, same time, same place, same lunch, more gossip. Bye.'

Sue was pleased for her two best friends, but couldn't help feeling a little left out having no new man to discuss. She'd split with her last boyfriend six months previously when she'd discovered he was two-timing her, and had been cautious ever since. Settling herself at her desk, she was immediately joined by Patsy, the office gossip, buzzing with the latest news.

'Have you met the new guy yet, Sue?'

'No, what's he like?'

'Quite dishy. He's from the New York office, apparently. My friend is in his department and told me he's 26, single, a real charmer, and his name's Jack. Sounds interesting. Wonder if we'll meet him?'

'I expect he'll be at the staff meeting on Friday. Now let me get on before my boss comes back. He wants this lot finished today, or I'll be out on my ear and not have a chance to check him out.'

Sue caught up with her work-load, and was surprised but pleased when Jack made a point of talking to her after the meeting, and finished by asking her out on a date. She'd have something to contribute when she met the girls for lunch after the weekend. Several weeks passed, and all three girls were happy in their new relationships.

'It's going great,' Kathy told them. 'The only odd thing is he can only see me on Mondays and Thursdays. There was a concert on Wednesday but he said he wasn't free other nights, so we couldn't go. He was a bit cagey about the reason, but I suppose I shouldn't moan.'

'That's odd,' Pam said. 'John took me to that concert. It was fantastic. Pity it was only for the one night, but I see him on Wednesdays and Saturdays so it worked out fine.'

'Did you go, Sue?'

'No, I see Jack on Tuesdays and Fridays. I'm getting a bad feeling about this.'

'What do you mean?'

'Well, think about it. Three Americans of the same age all turn up at the same time. None of us have met the other two's partners. I wonder what he does on Sundays?'

'He? You mean you think they're all the same guy?'

'Well, it does sound suspicious. How can we prove it though?'

'We need photos to compare.'

'Yes, and we could ask his date of birth. He might lie, but there's no reason why he should.'

Two weeks later three mouths dropped open when the girls all produced identical photos of the same man.

'I managed to get a peek at the date on his passport,' Kathy said. '27th October, 1992.'

'That's the same date John told me,' Pam added.

'Full house,' Sue said. 'I knew I shouldn't have trusted him.'

'So, what do we do now? I wish we could all turn up together somewhere and see his face.'

'Give him an ultimatum. Make it a Sunday, and tell him if he doesn't come, it's finished.'

'We could try, or just tell him we've rumbled his little game, and forget all about him,' Sue suggested.

'I want the satisfaction of making him squirm,' Pam said. 'Let's try the other way first.'

Before they had a chance to make a decision, there was a surprising turn of events. Their usual café closed for a week's holiday, and with no other place convenient for all three girls to meet during their lunch break, they didn't see each other during the last week of October.

'Pam, I know it's short notice but are you free tomorrow?' John asked her on their usual Saturday date. 'I've managed to wangle some cover, so some friends are getting together to celebrate my birthday. We're having a few drinks at The George, and we've got an extension to Sunday licensing hours as it's a private party. I'll pick you up at 8. Please say you can come. It wouldn't be the same without you.'

Pam still hadn't decided what to do about John, but thought it might be a good opportunity to find out more about him so decided to accept his invitation. When they arrived at the exclusive hotel, she made a quick trip to the ladies to freshen up, then went to look for him in the room reserved for the party. Spying him standing by the bar she went to join him, only to stop dead in her tracks when she noticed his companion. It was Kathy.

'You didn't tell me you were coming, Kathy,' she said, unsure how to handle the situation.

'I didn't expect to see you either, Pam. Let me introduce you to….'

'Hey, you two. Fancy seeing you here. What's going on?' It was Sue, holding onto the arm of her man, and gazing in amazement at her friend's boyfriend.

'There you are Pam. I see you've met the other two-thirds of the terrible trio,' John said as he came up behind her.

'It's not often we can all get together, but this is a special occasion. No problems with Mum, guys. I've just spoken to her and she's fine, and says to make the most of our evening. Back to the care rota tomorrow, but tonight it's time to party with our ladies.'

'Any requests for the DJ, girls?'

Sue, Pam and Kathy looked at the triplets, then answered in unison.

'There's only one option. "American Trilogy."'

Bed of roses.

It was Shakespeare who first said 'The course of true love never did run smooth.'

That's what he promised me. The good-looking charmer who left silly notes on my desk to make me smile. As the newbie in the office I assumed the other women were jealous of the attention he was paying me, and ignored their snide comments. He was everything a girl could ask for; tall, good looking, generous, funny and romantic.

He hit on me from the very first day, but not in a smarmy way. He seemed popular with all the staff, and I assumed he was including me in the banter to make me feel at home.

'Hey, Rose. You're joining us down the pub tonight, aren't you? Payday tradition, last Friday of the month. If you give me one of your beautiful smiles, I might even buy you a drink from my hard-earned wages.'

'Leave the girl alone,' Penny from accounts called back to him. 'She's probably got better things to do than start her weekend off in your company.'

I wasn't sure whether she didn't want me there, or was being supportive. In the midst of all the glamorous assistants, she was the only plain one, apart from me, of course. We were both overweight, but at least I had the height to carry it off. She was short and dumpy, and wore glasses all the time, whereas I only used them for driving. Still, she had been nice to me when I started, showing me where everything was, and taking me to the local sandwich bar on my first day.

'Are you going, Penny?' I asked.

'Yes, I usually get dragged along. I'm the only one with half a brain to sort out the bill.'

I noticed her glance at the other girls as she said it, and although she was smiling there was a barb in her voice, as if she was getting in a dig at their intelligence.

'OK. Why not? Give me ten minutes to cancel my hot date and I'll be ready.'

'We'll see you in there. I'll save you a seat,' Rick called as the rest of the crowd left together.

It was only a short walk to the pub, and Penny took the opportunity to have a private chat as we made our way there.

'What do you think of our Rick, then Rose?' she asked as we left the building.

'He seems pleasant enough,' I replied. 'What about you? Do you get on with him?'

'Oh, he's very good at his job. One of the best managers I've had. If you stick to work you'll be fine.'

I'd already decided she fancied him, but was curious if it had ever gone any further between them.

'He's not really my type but he's certainly good looking. Is he married?' I asked.

'He doesn't seem to be. He never mentions a wife, and at the Christmas party he always has a different lady on his arm. I think a few of the girls

16

have been out with him, but they never tell me anything about it, although I've heard them gossiping amongst themselves. This is the pub. Shall we go in?'

'Hey, Rose. Over here. I saved you a seat as I promised. Now, what are you drinking?'

Penny and I made our way through the already crowded bar, and I squeezed into the bench seat indicated, as Rick went to the bar to get my white wine spritzer. The others were on chairs around the table but when he returned he took the place next to me in the booth, so close I could feel the warmth of his leg brushing against mine.

I wasn't usually much of a drinker but that night I got tipsy and he ended up seeing me home in a cab. He was the perfect gentleman, escorting me to my door and giving me a friendly good night kiss before returning to the waiting taxi. On Monday morning I was a little nervous at facing everyone, but although I caught some of the bitches smirking, Rick was his usual self.

'What did you think of the pub? Not the most salubrious of places but it's local, so I guess we dropped into the habit of going there. Perhaps next time we can go somewhere nicer. I know a lovely place down by the river which does a great Sunday lunch.'

Before I could ask if he meant all the crowd or just the two of us, the senior manager called him into the office. He was sent away on a business trip for two weeks and on his return spent most of the time in meetings so I didn't get a chance to talk to him, although he always gave me a wink and a smile when he passed my desk.

I was transferred to another department, so wasn't sure if the invitation to the payday drink night still stood. If I went, it might give me a chance to get to know Rick better, but Friday afternoon I received an email from him.

"Sorry, can't make tonight. Explain later. Rick. x"

That decided me. There was no point in going if he wasn't going to be there, so it would be better to go straight home and spend the evening doing housework. That would leave my weekend free for my first love, gardening. When Penny popped her head in just before five, I made an excuse I had a date that night. I'd heard nothing more from Rick until, as I went to close down my computer, another message popped up.

"Sorry for the short notice. Free Sunday? Pick you up at your place around 12 for lunch? Rick. x"

For a moment I wondered how he knew my address until I remembered he had taken me home, so after sending a quick reply, *"Fine. See you then,"* I left work in a tizz, already trying to decide what to wear.

He arrived right on time with a beautiful bouquet of flowers, the food was perfect, the company amazing, and I couldn't help noticing the number of envious glances sent our way by the other female diners. Once again I drank a little too much, so it seemed natural to invite him in for coffee when he took me home. It was a beautiful summer evening and he admired the roses in my garden as we sat on the patio enjoying the warmth of the evening.

He stayed the night and although I was inexperienced, his love making was wonderful. I woke around three to his whispered "Goodbye," before falling asleep to dreams of happy ever after. I bounced into work on Monday morning but my good mood was shattered when, from inside the toilet cubicle, I overheard Camilla and Sandra discussing me.

'Did you hear? He won his bet. All the boys are talking about it.'

'What did you expect? Rick could charm the knickers off a nun, and it's not as if she would have many other offers, is it?'

Unsure whether to believe them I sent Rick a message saying I needed to talk to him urgently. He came round and admitted everything. Afterwards he explained how sorry he was and begged me to forgive him.

That was nearly a year ago. Now it's definitely a bed of roses.

After I chopped him up and put him in the compost bin the roses are coming up beautifully.

Blind date.

They say that Love is blind.

I don't know why Emma was so nervous. She was a beautiful girl who loved meeting new people, and had such a radiant personality everyone was immediately drawn to her. As her best friend, I had spent the past hour helping her go through her wardrobe, trying to select the perfect outfit for her blind date later that evening.

'If you don't make your mind up soon, you'll be so late he'll have stood you up anyway,' I said, trying to chivvy her along.

'I know, but this is so important. "You only get the first chance to make a last impression," or whatever it is they say. What do you think Sandy?'

I couldn't help laughing when I noticed her Labrador was cocking his head to one side, and seemed to be studying her intently before giving his opinion. *"Woof,"* he barked.

'There you are then,' I joked, 'two against one. That dress is perfect; the blue matches your eyes, now get a move on.'

An hour later Emma was ready, and putting Sandy into the back seat I drove her to the restaurant. We had agreed that I would pick her up about eleven, and I would phone her at 9.30, so if the meeting was a total disaster, she could make an excuse to escape.

I was on tenterhooks wondering how it was going until my mobile rang about 9.15, breaking me out of my reverie. 'Hi. It's me. Don't bother to phone me, he's great. We've found so much to talk about, the food is perfect and we've got the same sense of humour. I've just dived into the ladies to ring you. See you at 11. Got to get back or he'll wonder where I've got to. Thanks for everything. Bye.'

With that she was gone, and I was left holding the dead phone in my hand without having been able to get a word in edgeways. At least she sounded happy, so I had no worries on that score.

On the drive home she didn't talk much, which was unusual for my normally garrulous bestie. She just sat there with a soppy look on her face and I let her be, assuming she was exhausted from the excitement of the day.

Over the following few weeks I began to feel slightly hurt, and upset that we were drifting apart. Emma didn't phone me so much, except to confirm details where I had previously agreed to give her a lift to her appointments. Even then most of her conversation revolved around "him," and I began to feel more like a chauffeur than a friend.

Months passed, and instead of our almost daily phone calls and weekly meetings, most of our communication relied on text messages via her adapted phone. I had still not met her boyfriend, although I had seen happy, smiling photos on social media of them at the beach, in the garden or meeting with friends. I felt rejected.

One day I gave myself a good talking-to. Was I jealous? No, I don't think so. Was I happy for her? Yes, she deserved a good man after all she had been through. We had been friends since junior school, and it was only when she was in her 20s that the disaster struck and changed her life. I had been there for her then, and I would continue to be there for her now, ten years later, even if it was only in the background.

They say you can go months without speaking to a special friend, but then you carry on as if it was yesterday. Even though I hadn't heard from Emma for weeks, when I got the message that her operation was confirmed for next month, I immediately replied 'Do you want a lift?'

Her answer, 'I know I've been neglecting you, but I really want you to be there' was enough. We sorted out the arrangements, and although it felt odd to do it by texts rather than speaking directly, I was happy she wanted me with her.

I put the date in my diary and arranged to take the time off work. Logging onto my laptop the night before the big day, I was surprised to receive a message from "him." He apologised for intruding, but knowing we both cared for Emma, hoped we could provide mutual support while we were waiting for her results.

The next day I picked her up to drive her to the hospital, and it was like the intervening months had never existed. We carried on our conversation as if it was only a few hours since we had last spoken. I felt we were the same close friends, sharing the same secrets we had in our teens.

Just before she was wheeled off to the operating room, I hugged her and joked, 'I'll see you soon, and you'll see me.'

It was a long, emotional evening waiting for the results, but sharing the trepidation with her boyfriend, and realising he really loved her, made the time pass more quickly. Eventually the night staff kicked us out and told us to come back the next morning. Even though I was there early, I saw him enter the private room just before I did.

Despite still being woozy from the anaesthetic Emma smiled at us. 'Moment of truth' she said, as the medical staff slowly unwound the bandages from her eyes.

'At last I can see you both,' she whispered with a break in her voice. 'Not only have I got my sight back, but the first people I see are my blind date and my best friend, the two people I love the most. Who says Love is blind?'

Chocolate love story.

Chocolates and love somehow seem to go well together.

'There's something I've always wanted to ask you.'

'Yes, what is it? You know I keep no secrets from you.'

'Why are you such a beautiful brown colour when your Mother was white?'

'My ancestors were dark, developing under the blazing sun along the Amazon for 4,000 years, and taking in the goodness from the life-giving rays. Nearly 500 years ago we arrived in Spain where we were the guests of Royalty.

'My forefathers were even used as currency; a slave could be bought for 100, the services of a prostitute for 10, and 4 got you a rabbit for dinner. 170 years ago we arrived in England, and our shape was changed from a fluid drink to a solid slab.

Despite their differences my parents determined to be together. In Switzerland my pure white mother's milk was sweetened and condensed. Finally, she was joined with my dusky father to produce the beauty who now stands before you.'

'Such a fascinating tale, but there is one thing you forgot to mention.'

'And what is that?'

'You also taste good. Parting is such sweet sorrow. Yum, yum.

'Adios my sweet chocolate chunk.'

Dance to the end of Love.

A 1984 song released by Leonard Cohen, but I was surprised to learn his inspiration was the Holocaust.

For old times' sake I decided to pay one last visit to the small taverna where we had first met. It was when I was young and experiencing my first taste of freedom without parental control. Five girls, full of life, seduced by the sun, the relaxed atmosphere and the romance of sitting at midnight listening to music in the warm breeze, all ready and willing to fall in love under the twinkling foreign stars.

The swarthy Lotharios swarmed like bees around a honeypot, and we were enchanted by the local guys, so unlike the ones we knew back home. Even Jenny fell for their charms, despite her marriage to her childhood sweetheart less than six months before.

Jackie flirted and had fun, but made sure she slept alone in her own bed. The sisters, Paula and

Patricia watched out for each other, and hooked up with two English lads, brothers who were staying at our hotel. Both insisted it was more than a holiday fling, and in some ways they were right. Paula married Mike, had two children and they recently celebrated their silver wedding anniversary, and the birth of their first grandchild. Patricia married his brother John, but five years later they were divorced, which must have made joint family celebrations difficult.

I enjoyed myself but was too sensible to give my heart away to the many local lads who told me I was beautiful and swore undying love. Tony was different, watching over me like a big brother, and rescuing me when I found myself in a sticky situation. He served behind the bar in the evenings, helped out in the kitchen when they were busy, and was always there when I called in mid-morning for a coffee.

I discovered he took a fifteen-minute break around eleven, and got into the habit of arriving ten minutes beforehand so he could share my table.

Although I think he was attracted to me he never made it obvious, but when we were alone we discussed our hopes and dreams for the future.

His ambition was to procure formal training as a chef and open his own restaurant, preferably in London. I admitted my dream of running my own business, and told him about the evening classes I attended after work to learn the necessary skills.

In the evenings, when the fairy lights came on and the tables were set outside, a musician sang and played romantic music to entertain the tourists and the older locals. Although Tony was busy serving drinks, I was happy to sit and listen while my friends went off to the discos and clubs more suitable to the younger set. When the last guest had gone, he would put on some quiet music and we would dance until the early hours.

Like all good things the holiday came to an end, and for a while we kept in touch. After a few years I graduated with my diploma in business studies, and although at first it was hard going, eventually I managed to set up and run my own successful business. I heard from Tony that he was leaving the island, and going to study under a famous chef in Paris. He promised to send his new address once he was settled, but I moved house at the same time, and although I sent a letter to the taverna giving him my new details it remained unanswered.

Five years passed, and through the business I accidentally met the love of my life. We married, had three children, and in between achieved our ambitions. We were there for each other, supportive in the bad times and sharing the joy in the good ones. We were comfortably off, successful in our chosen careers, and yet, and yet….

Something was missing. With our hectic life-styles we hardly saw each other as we both jetted off to different destinations for important conferences. It became a standing joke that we needed our secretaries to book an appointment for our next meeting. Our last communication had been by Skype, as it often was these days. Even then, he was interrupted as we went to say goodbye.

'Sorry, sweetheart. Something urgent has come up. Got to go. Bye,' he said as the connection was cut. No "miss you," no "see you soon." Had we reached the end of love?

Was that the reason I found myself here, in the quiet of winter, leaning over the rail to gaze at the beach below? It was very different now. The quaint old-fashioned shops had been replaced by modern glass and concrete shopping malls, the tiny restaurants and cafes by international, familiar chains.

Was it the salt spray or a stray tear I wiped away from my cheek? As my vision cleared, I noticed a small hut below me, almost hidden by the rocks. It couldn't be, could it? Was there any way the taverna could have survived the ravages of progress? It looked the same, but further back on the shore from where I remembered, but it had been twenty-five years, and memory can be a funny thing.

Despite my unsuitable shoes I determined to find out, and picked my way carefully down the broken stone steps until I was facing the rear staff entrance where I used to wait for Tony to take his break. Suddenly, tiny coloured lights came on, transforming the run-down beach shack into the romantic rendezvous I remembered. Unbelievably the sound of music drifted towards me as the door opened and a man emerged, carrying a small table and two chairs.

Although his dark hair was flecked with grey, he was unmistakable as Tony, the man who had stolen my heart at first sight, who I had met by chance several years later, and whose ring I had been wearing for more than twenty years.

'I'm glad you came,' he smiled. 'I would have looked a bit stupid dancing by myself. Happy anniversary darling.'

As he took me in his arms, and I listened to the words of our song, I knew the dance would end long before our love did.

Follow me. Christmas Eve.

You might not realise this is a song title, but I was inspired to write this story after listening to the song by Vernon and the GIs, recorded in 2011.

I met her at a Christmas party. They were not usually my kind of thing but my workmates nagged me into it. Just to keep in the spirit of the season, I agreed to go for an hour or so before I made my excuses and adjourned to the pub for a quiet pint.

I knew I had made a mistake when the invitation showed the dress code as formal attire for the gentlemen, and carriages at 1 a.m. By then it was too late, so I hired a penguin suit and resigned myself to an evening of boredom, vowing never again.

The twelve-seater mini-bus hired for the occasion deposited us on the pavement in front of a swanky West End hotel, and immediately hired flunkies rushed to usher us inside, waiting for their tip.

37

Don't get me wrong, I'm not tight. It's just that paying for common courtesy goes against all I believe in. My first impressions were correct as we entered a gaudy ballroom, drank overpriced fizz, ate things on sticks from the trays of passing waiters, and made small talk.

Eventually we were directed into the dining area, and after giving our names were seated at large, round tables with strangers. It seems it was a deliberate policy to split up groups to 'enhance the friendly atmosphere.'

My immediate neighbour was a self-made man with a fortune, as he explained to me within five minutes of meeting him. On his other side was an expensively dressed lady, and I use the word in its loosest sense, with a low-cut dress and a false, giggly laugh. They were well suited.

Once he had established that I wasn't a suitable contact for his social circle he ignored me, and spent all his time flirting with her. The seat to my left was empty. I wasn't sure if I was pleased or not. On the one hand it meant I didn't have to listen to banal conversation, on the other it meant I had no-one to talk to, which would make the hours drag even more.

The first course was served, something cheffy and artistic but not what you would actually call food. I was sorely tempted to excuse myself and disappear, knowing my absence would probably not even be noticed.

Just at that moment a waiter settled a lady, and this time I'm not being sarcastic, into the chair next to me, and I turned to see the most gorgeous woman I have ever seen in my life. She wasn't traditionally beautiful, her nose was a bit too big, her hair was windswept and her face was flushed.

Apologising for being late, she gave me a smile to melt any man's heart. She laughed when I said she hadn't missed much, just as the waiters returned to serve our main course. Glancing at my plate, the disdain must have shown on my face. She looked at her meal, and we both got a fit of the giggles.

Although we didn't eat much, the evening improved no end and we stuck it out for another hour until a really dire band started up. In my spare time I was a singer in a Rock and Roll band, and when they had finishing massacring one of my favourite songs, I looked at her and said, 'I've had enough. Follow me?'

In an instant she replied, 'I'll get my coat. See you outside in five minutes.'

That was it; from then on we were inseparable. The following Christmas my gift to her was an engagement ring. After I had got down on one knee and slipped it onto her finger, she accepted my proposal and made me the happiest man in the world.

'I've got something for you too,' she said as she took my hand, 'Follow me.'

On Christmas morning we woke to the sound of church bells, and that's when we decided to get married at Christmas the following year.

Winter turned into summer and before we knew it autumn had arrived. We walked hand in hand through the falling leaves making arrangements for when we would be together forever.

That winter was one of the hardest on record, but we stuck to our plans for our wedding on Christmas Eve. Even if some of our friends were snow-bound and unable to get to the ceremony, the important thing was we would be together. Christmas day would see us as husband and wife in the new house we had bought.

I had been living there for a few months, but she was temporarily renting digs up North, until she finished her work contract and travelled down to join me. My main concern was that the weather would hinder her transport plans, but she phoned me as she was boarding the coach.

'I'm on my way. I can't wait to follow you down South, and start our life together. The coach should get into London sometime early evening. Tomorrow is Christmas Eve, when we can stop following each other and just be together. I can't wait to see you. Love you.'

Keeping with tradition she was staying in a London hotel on the day before our wedding, so I wouldn't see her until we took our vows in church. Even so I checked my mobile every few minutes waiting for her message that she had arrived safely, and was now going to catch up with some sleep so she would look her best when we exchanged rings.

For the sake of something to do I switched on the television and watched the news. It was all about the horrendous weather, cancelled trains and videos of cars slipping and sliding on the ice.

As I went to turn it off and get some sleep, I caught a news flash about a major crash on the MI. A coach had skidded on the ice causing a multiple pile-up. Bit by bit the details emerged, and I sat up all night until finally they published an emergency contact number for friends and relatives.

When my messages and calls to my fiancée's mobile went unanswered, I eventually managed to get through to the emergency number. I tried not to snap when they asked if I was a relative, but finally my desperation must have got through when I explained we were due to be married the following day.

'I'm very sorry. That name has been identified as one of the people who didn't survive.'

I put down the phone as the operator was still talking, giving information about the hospital the bodies had been taken to and offering her sympathy.

Early morning on Christmas Eve I woke to find the television still on, and my neck aching from where I had finally fallen asleep in the chair. I spent the day in a daze, thinking this was to have been my wedding day, but unable to motivate myself to let people know, or cancel the arrangements.

Just as dusk was falling, I woke from a trance-like sleep, and glancing out of the window noticed the snow was still falling and a bitter wind was blowing. Nothing mattered now, although I did grab a thick coat before setting off to the local cemetery.

As it was Christmas, the gates were still open for people to lay their tributes for their loved ones, although there was no-one about. Despite the cold, I wandered about aimlessly until I found myself in the neglected, older part of the grounds. The graves on the newer part of the cemetery all held floral accolades, but here there was nobody left to remember the ones who had gone to meet their maker a hundred years or more before.

Even the carving on the tombstones had faded with the years, so the names could no longer be read. I sat down between two overgrown memorials and huddled into my overcoat. The sound of church bells woke me, and I realised that no-one had thought to check this part of the cemetery when they locked up to enjoy their family Christmas.

I wasn't worried. I had nothing to go home to, and no reason to leave even if I was blue and shivering. What did I care about hyperthermia if there was no warm body to bring me to my senses?

At first I couldn't make out the words, but gradually my senses returned from a semi-comatose state and I recognised my Darling, dressed in her wedding gown, walking up the aisle of the church towards me. The choir sang, and our friends were smiling until she stopped, turned, and made her way back towards the door of the chapel.

The snow was falling again as I saw her leave the church and glide back towards the cemetery.

'Wait,' I cried. 'Come back. Please don't leave me.'

Then I heard her voice calling softly, 'I'm here my love. Follow me.'

From this day forward.

Young or old, Love doesn't care.

Dear Mary.

Will you be my girlfriend?

Billy (aged 6 ¾).

Dear Billy.

No. Boys are nasty and silly.

Mary.

Hi Mary.

Do you remember me? We used to be in Miss Wood's class in infant's school. I bumped into your sister and she gave me your new address. I'm in Watling street, not far away from you. Perhaps we could meet up sometime, and catch up. Say hello to your parents and give me your phone number if you like.

Hi Billy.

Only if you promise not to pull my pigtails. Not that I've got any now. They don't suit nearly 17-year-olds. My phone number is at the top of this letter. Give me a call.

My Dearest Mary.

I'm not allowed to say too much, but it's not a bundle of laughs here. Perhaps I should have gone into the bank as Dad suggested, rather than join the forces, but your letters always cheer me up. I can't wait to get home and see you again. When I do, I've something important to ask you.

Darling Billy.

It's just as well you're away. Since that wonderful romantic evening when you proposed, all the talk here is about bridesmaids' dresses, flowers and whether we should invite great aunt Aggie. I can imagine how much you'd enjoy that! Just make sure you're there for the big day. Love you. X

Mary, my sweetheart.

I can't wait to make you my wife and love you forever. Aunt Aggie is your department, but I promise I will never let you down. All my love always.

Your soon to be husband Billy. X

Hello, Mister.

This is your Mrs. It still feels funny saying that but what a wonderful day it was when we exchanged our vows. I'm counting down the days until you're home again, and I have some special news to tell you. Remember your last leave? I shouldn't tell you in a letter but I'm so excited. Stay safe my love and hurry home.

Your loving wife Mary. X

Hello Mary.

How are you and the nippers getting on without me? I expect you're pleased I'm not under your feet when you're trying to be the perfect mum. I know you; little Miss Independent, always trying to prove you can cope without me. This contract should be finished within a couple of weeks, and I'll be home to sort out the long list of jobs you'll have lined up for me. I can imagine you laughing and calling me a chauvinist pig, but you know it's true.

Anyway, sweetheart, it'll be worth it in the long run when they pay me the enormous bonus for setting up their company, and we'll be rich.

Well, maybe not millionaires, but there should be enough to put the deposit on that house you've set your heart on. When I get home we'll arrange for the parents to baby sit, and I'll wine you and dine you like the young lovers we used to be before the kids arrived. Find somewhere nice and book it. Never mind the expense. Love you.

Billy. x

Huh! Typical man.

Gives his order and expects the dutiful little wife to make all the arrangements. OK mister. You asked for it. Our sixth wedding anniversary will be spent at the Boutique Hotel and Spa. I've arranged for the bridal suite with candlelit dinner and overnight stay. Mum and dad will have the monsters for the night and champagne will flow like water. Love you Billy. I hope it'll be worth it. I know how hard you work and I do miss you. Once you've read this letter it will self-destruct. Can't have you thinking your soon to be thirty-year-old wife is getting soft in her old age.

Mary. X

Hi sweetheart.

What a fantastic weekend. Worth every penny, even if I did have to take on another project in the middle of nowhere to pay for it. Still, at least it's only a few weeks, although it's poor timing with everything going on. What did the surveyor say about the house? Have you heard from the mortgage company yet? Let me know if they need any more information about my income and I'll ask payroll to send it asap. Love you.

Billy. X

Hello Darling.

Which do you want first? The good news, or the "not sure how you'll take it but other good news?" Survey was fine. Only a few minor bits, which we expected with an older house. Structurally sound, might need a new roof in four or five years' time, but nothing major. The mortgage has been agreed in principle, which is great as we'll need the space for a family of five. Yes, you heard me right. We're expecting an anniversary present from our weekend away. Hurry home. We've things to discuss. Love you.

M. x

    Hello Mary.

I'm getting too old for this lark, always flying all over the world and missing seeing the kids growing up. Can't believe our Janie will be eighteen soon. Has she made a decision about Uni yet? Just when I think we can start splashing out a bit on us, another expense comes up. Still, we can't begrudge her a decent education, and the pension pot is building up nicely. Think of the fun we'll have when we both retire. Love the gym photo of you with pigtails. Brought back memories of when we were young. You're still as adorable.

Billy. x

    Hi Darling.

Did you ever notice how we've always had to share important news by letter, instead of hearing it together? Well, how do you fancy being a granddad? Mark and Katy are expecting; thankfully the baby's due about six weeks before

Paul's wedding. At least when Janie has her engagement party you'll be office based, and have finished dashing all over the world. No doubt you'll expect your dinner on the table when you get off the 6 o'clock commute, and want me catering to your every whim. Still love you, even if we're now both officially old.

M. x

Fantastic news, Darling.

I can't say I haven't enjoyed travelling, but at the same time I've missed being able to spend my everyday life with you, and watching our babies grow into fully grown up human beings. Should I start calling you grandma? Don't answer that. I think I know your answer. Another month and I'll be around every evening and weekend to drive you mad. Don't let the children book us up for too much babysitting. We need time for us.

Love as always Billy. x

My dearest Billy.

In all our years together, this is the hardest letter I've ever had to write. It seems daft when I know

you'll be home soon, but since the doctor phoned this afternoon, I've been reminiscing about our forty-four years of married life. You've always been my rock and my strength, but for one reason or another, somehow every momentous occasion was communicated by letter. It's not good news. When you get home, don't say anything, just give me a hug. Until death us do part. Love you.
Mary. x

My dearest, darling, love of my life.
I can't believe you've gone, but you will always be with me, here in my heart. This final goodbye letter on your gravestone comes with a bunch of your favourite carnations. They might die, but my love never will. Do they have pens and paper for writing from heaven?
Billy. xxxxxxxxxxxx

Ghost story – The wedding.

Love is often associated with weddings, but perhaps not so much with ghosts.

Not many ghost stories start with a wedding- but mine did.

It was love at first sight, I saw him, thought "Wow," kept trying to catch his eye across the crowded dance floor, then got a little tipsy when he didn't even spare me a second glance. There seemed to be thousands of people at my best friend's wedding, and I lost sight of him among the throng. Throwing myself into the spirit of the party, I was soon up dancing and strutting my stuff with the best of them.

It turned into a great evening. I flirted with the best man, and even gave him my number to call me when I get home, although I made sure I left him at my hotel room door with just a goodnight kiss. I wasn't that drunk. Several of the guests were staying overnight rather than face the long journey home, and there were a few bleary-eyed faces when we staggered down to breakfast the next morning. Looking round the dining room I hoped to catch sight of my mysterious man, but there was no sign of him. Even though I tried to be subtle, most of my friends caught my interest in him, although nobody seemed to know who he was.

It wasn't until two weeks later when Jackie returned from her honeymoon that I was able to arrange to meet her for lunch, and try to sound her out for more information. Not surprisingly, when we met all she wanted to talk about was her new husband and her wonderful new home, and show me the wedding photos. It was while we were browsing through them that I saw right at the back, in one of the crowd scenes a face I recognised.

'Who's that?' I asked, pointing him out. 'I remember seeing him at the wedding but he disappeared early.'

Jackie glanced where I was pointing then suddenly went white. 'I don't know,' she said, 'perhaps he was a friend of Dave's. Anyway, how about another drink?'

Even though our glasses were still half full she jumped up to the bar, and when she returned put away the album, and started talking about how wonderful Jamaica was. I was sure she had deliberately changed the subject, and wondered for a moment if he had been an old flame she didn't want to talk about.

After that I didn't see much of her, and when I phoned she just made excuses about being busy with the house and her new husband. Although I knew she now had other responsibilities, I couldn't help feeling hurt at the way she was cutting me out of her life. Apart from the occasional e-mail, the next time I heard from her was an invitation to her baby-shower. All the gang would be there and I felt obliged to join them. It was to be held in the same hotel where she had celebrated her wedding, and once again most of us were staying overnight.

This time it was ladies only, and although the rest of us helped to drink the bar dry, Jackie stuck to orange juice in view of her condition and retired early. About a dozen of us settled in for a good gossip in the cosy hotel lounge after she left, and in our mellow state conversation turned to our love lives, partners and plans for the future.

I had started seeing Joe fairly regularly, but although he wanted to make it a more serious relationship, somehow for me the spark was not there. I enjoyed his company and his friendship but didn't want to take it any further. Maybe I was being stupid but it was the tall, dark-haired man I had seen at the wedding who still haunted my dreams and fantasies.

Several of the girls knew I had hooked up with Joe at the reception, and teased me about the next wedding being mine. That was when I made the decision to break it off between us. I knew I wasn't being fair to him, and couldn't help noticing Penny's interest when I said we were just friends. It was also when I realised my life was a mess and I needed to get out of the rut I had fallen into.

At three in the morning we decided to call it a night, and made our way back to our respective hotel rooms. As I had only decided to attend at the last minute, I wasn't in the main block with the others, but off a corridor in the annex, in the oldest part of the hotel.

Bidding the others goodnight, I left the modern well-lit area and tried to remember the way back to my room. The archway almost hidden behind the old-fashioned fireplace looked familiar, and led me into a gloomy passageway, half lit by electric candles in old fashioned wall sconces. When I had checked in, all the connecting doorways had been open but now I noticed signs saying *"Fire exit"* and the heavy oak partitions were firmly closed, invoking a peculiar feeling of claustrophobia.

Is was also eerily silent, and for a moment I considered going back the way I had come and asking someone from reception to point me in the right direction. Opening one last door, I breathed a sigh of relief when I saw a sign on the wall showing the direction to my room.

Walking along a dead-end with my suite in sight, I jumped when I noticed a shadowy figure emerge from behind an old-fashioned aspidistra in a large pot at the far end of the corridor. The scream that rose in my throat died when I recognised the man I had been lusting over for months in my dreams.

'I knew you would come back,' he said in a deep sexy voice as I stood there gaping.

'Who are you?' I stuttered. 'What are you doing here?'

'My name is Adam,' he smiled, 'and I live here. Welcome back, Julia.'

'How do you know my name? You didn't even notice me at Jackie's wedding. What were you doing there anyway?'

'I attend all the weddings held here. You could say it's my job, has been for years.'

'You mean you're a waiter or something,' I asked, which brought a wry smile in response.

'Something like that. This was the home of my ancestors, and I sort of stayed on when it was turned into a hotel. In fact, the room you have been allocated used to be my own chambers. You might have noticed this is the old part of the original building. Did you have a nice evening with your friend?'

'Yes, it was good. She seems very happy to be starting a family. Where were you earlier? I didn't see you.'

'Yes, it's a shame he's such a bullying shit who will treat her badly. Maybe it will be for the best when she loses the baby. I was there. I'm always there, but like a good waiter most of the time I'm invisible. I do what needs to be done and try not to get noticed. It's only a selected few who actually see me. That's why I couldn't acknowledge you at the wedding. I had to wait until the right moment, and here we are.'

It was surreal and I wondered if I had drunk more than I thought. My hand was shaking so much I couldn't get the old-fashioned key in the lock, until Adam took it off me and easily opened the door, ushering me into the room.

I was not surprised when he followed me in, although I noticed he left the key in the lock after he had closed it behind us. I should have felt scared at this stranger intruding into my personal space, but for some reason I felt completely safe in his company.

Looking perfectly at home he made me a hot drink from the hospitality tray, strong black coffee, no sugar, exactly how I liked it, then raiding the mini bar accompanied it with a shot of Sambuca, before taking a seat on the sofa next to me.

'You know Joe was never right for you. I'm glad you made the decision to end it. He and Penny will be celebrating their own wedding here next year. You were right to give them the opportunity to be together. In fifty years' time they will be back with their children and grandchildren to celebrate their Golden wedding anniversary.'

'And what about me? Where will I be in fifty years' time?' I asked quietly.

'Why, here with me of course, where you belong.'

I was too surprised to answer, but didn't resist when he gently pulled me into his arms and kissed me passionately. The rest of the night passed in a haze of love-making until I woke the next morning feeling sore but contented, to find myself alone.

Perhaps too much drink and nostalgia had caused the erotic dream. Noticing the time, I showered and dressed quickly and made my way down to breakfast. The others were already there as I took the last remaining seat between Jackie and Penny. Neither were very talkative, and it felt strange remembering what Adam had said about Jackie losing the baby, and Penny having a happy life with Joe.

Obviously, I kept my thoughts to myself, and most of the girls assumed I was feeling fragile after drinking too much the night before. Once we had finished eating, we made our way back to our respective rooms to gather our things before meeting up in the foyer to say our goodbyes. The trip back along the corridors seemed quicker and much less daunting than it had the night before, although I hesitated outside the door to my room when I found it unlocked.

'Good Morning, Madam. I'm sorry. I thought you were still in the dining room. I can come back later to make up the room.'

'No, it's no problem. I've just come back to collect my things then I'll be checking out.'

'If you're sure. I hope you slept well. It's a beautiful room isn't it, even if it is supposed to be haunted.'

'Yes, it's lovely. What's the story about the ghost?'

'Well, as you will have noticed, this room is part of the original hotel that dates back to the 17th century. The story goes that a tall, handsome man whose family owned the estate, was betrothed to marry a beautiful local girl. On their wedding day his fiancée Julia never turned up, and he spent the rest of his days confined to the hotel and never left it again. Anyway, it makes for a good story. I hope we will see you again.'

'Yes, I'm sure you will. Thank you. Goodbye.'

Pulling my suitcase behind me, I returned to the reception area deep in thought. There were the usual rounds of hugs and kisses, and promises to keep in touch as gradually everyone dispersed to catch their trains or taxis home.

Penny pulled me to one side, and although hesitant to say what was on her mind eventually spat it out. 'Julia, were you serious when you said you and Joe were only friends? I know he's very fond of you and I wouldn't want to muscle in if you are serious about each other.'

'Go for it, Penny. He's a great bloke, just not for me. I'm sure you'll be very happy together. Don't forget to invite me to your Golden wedding.'

She blushed scarlet, then with another hug promised to keep in touch and left, leaving just Jackie and me.

'I owe you an apology, Julia. I know I've not been a very good friend to you since I got married, but there have been some complications. It's been hard for Dave to give up his bachelor life-style, and now with the baby coming I haven't had much time for him. I always feel so tired and our sex life has become almost non-existent. I'm sure once she's born things will get back to normal and we'll be fine. Please forgive me and keep in touch. I really miss our girlie chats. Don't forget me, and thanks so much for coming. It wouldn't have been the same without you here.'

With that she gave me another hug and went out to her waiting cab. I felt a bit spooked. The conversations I had had with my friends seemed to confirm everything Adam had said. Maybe he didn't really exist and my subconscious had just tuned into the vibes from knowing my friends so well.

Picking up my overnight bag, I paid my bill and made my way to the station to catch my train home. Work the next day went from bad to worse, and after a particularly nasty argument with my boss I plucked up courage and handed in my notice. Now I was committed and only had a month to find myself a new job.

Unfortunately, the following week a major local employer unexpectedly went bankrupt, and the job centre was flooded with office managers looking for work. I was beginning to despair when I saw an agency advertising for a live-in administrator's position. At the same time my lease came up for review, and my landlady told me she needed my flat as her niece was returning from Australia to live with her.

I contacted the agency, had the interview and got the job. Although I didn't know much about it the salary was good, the hours reasonable and it was in a town I knew about twenty miles away, so I accepted the offer there and then. After a few days I received the confirmation letter with full details. It was at the hotel where I had celebrated Jackie's wedding and baby shower. It seemed I would be returning quicker than I expected.

Reporting for duty a few weeks later, I was shown my office at the rear of reception where I would be responsible for keeping the web site up to date, tracking logistics of visitors and assisting with the marketing of the hotel. Very occasionally I would be required to help out on the check-in desk but my hours would be nine to five, with Sundays and Thursdays free, meals would be provided and I would have my own private suite in the hotel. It was only when I was given the same room I had stayed in previously, that I had some second thoughts. The owner explained that some visitors had felt uncomfortable being so far away from the main foyer, and it had been decided that the rooms in the old part of the hotel would be allocated to staff, leaving the modern part for guests.

The rest of the staff were welcoming and helpful so I decided to make the best of it. I settled into my new home and always slept soundly, without any unwelcome intrusions. By Christmas, when I had been there three months I felt totally at home, as if this had always been my dream job. My marketing ideas were appreciated and implemented, and I was happy to see the occupancy rates steadily rising. The owners must have thought so too, as my December pay packet included a handsome bonus, with a personal thank you for my contribution to the success of the hotel.

New Year's Eve we had our most successful party ever. Although it was hard work, all the visitors enjoyed themselves and the compliments came thick and fast from contented guests, with nearly all of them enquiring about booking for the following year as they had had such a great time.

At three in the morning I made my way back along the now familiar corridors, happy that the evening had been such a success but ready for my bed.

I unlocked my door, still with the same old-fashioned key, only to be startled when a familiar sexy voice came from out of the darkness.

'Welcome home Darling. A toast to us Julia. Happy New Year and here's to our next fifty years together.'

It seemed my fate was sealed as I joined him in the toast to our pre-ordained future.

Golden girls of Malta.

I've had some wonderful holidays with the girls, both in Malta and other countries. Secrets!

Right. That was it. All over now.

Despite 26 years together, three children and a grandchild on the way, he had finally packed his bags and left. Gone off with his young floozy. Good Luck to him.

The house had been sold and I was due to move out in a couple of weeks into a two-bedroomed flat. The new place was close by, so I wouldn't miss seeing all my old friends. It was in a better area and nearer to town.

He was moving over forty miles away so we were unlikely to bump into each other much. The sale proceeds of the house had been split evenly, he was taking the horrible moggy who hated me, and the kids all had their own places. My only regret was that I hadn't kicked him out years ago.

My friends had regularly tried to get me to join them when they met up in Malta for a girlie holiday, but I had always refused. Although we all kept in touch by e-mail, Facebook and phone, it was difficult to arrange get-togethers as we lived some way away from each other. The holidays were the perfect way of getting together for a gossip, catch-up and to let our hair down without the encumbrances of children, husbands and daily routines.

When they came back, I always listened with envy to their tales, admired their suntans and wished I could have been with them. Several times I had been on the point of booking but somehow Jim had always stopped me. He would suddenly announce he had to be away for an important business conference that week and we couldn't leave the house empty, tell me we couldn't afford it, or there would be a family emergency or social gathering we had to attend.

Thinking back, I realised the "conferences" were probably opportunities to be with his fancy piece and that it was just a form of bullying. Well this time nothing was going to stop me. I had my passport, sufficient cash and as a free-lance illustrator no problem with arranging time off work. I had checked the availability of the hotel where the girls would be staying, and found a good deal for the week they would be there. The only minor problem was that the flight for the Saturday they were due to arrive was fully booked. I had the option of going on the previous Thursday or making the long journey up north to another airport.

As all my previous holidays had been taken with my ex or the family, I had never travelled alone before. "Well, I'm a big girl now," I thought as I pressed the confirm button for the Thursday flight. I was sure I could survive being on my own for two days before the girls arrived. I intended to surprise them and hadn't actually let them know I would be joining them this year, although I had asked them for details of when and where they would be staying.

My suitcase was packed, and I had checked for the hundredth time that passport, flight confirmation, Euros, cash, credit card and other documentation was readily available in my flight bag. The sound of my mobile ringing made me jump. It was the cab driver announcing his presence outside. As I opened the door, he hurried forward to help me with my luggage and I was off on my adventure.

He was a chatty, friendly man and the hour's trip to the airport passed quickly. He found me a trolley; I paid the fare and then made my way to the check-in. There were only a few people in front of me and before I knew it, I had my boarding pass and an hour to spare before the departure gate was announced.

"Start as you mean to go on," I decided as I ordered a glass of wine to wash down my snack in the restaurant. A quick browse of the shops, a trip to the ladies, and a glance at the departure board told me it was time to make my way to Gate 15 for boarding. Settling in my aisle seat I noticed a tall, distinguished, grey-haired man in his fifties making his way towards me. Eat your heart out

George Clooney, he was gorgeous. His smile as I stood up to allow him into the window seat was to die for.

Unfortunately, just as he leaned over to introduce himself, an elderly Maltese lady took the seat between us making conversation difficult. I loved flying but soon discovered she had a fear of taking off and landing. I spent the first twenty minutes holding her hand and reassuring her while she chatted away to me in perfect, although heavily accented English.

As they started serving the mid-day meal the air hostess leaned over to speak to her. It seemed the flight was not full, and they had found her another seat with her family a few rows behind. With hugs and thanks and maximum commotion she eventually removed herself, and I found myself looking into the smiling face of "George" with only an empty seat between us.

'That's better,' he said as he leaned across to shake my hand. 'I'm Paul, pleased to meet you properly. I think you have a friend for life with the old lady. It was nice the way you helped her to overcome her fears, but I'm pleased she moved as it gives me the chance to get to know you.'

'Melita, usually known as "Mel." Hi Paul, nice to meet you too.'

The three-hour flight passed in a flash as we chatted, flirted and got to know each other. This holiday was starting with a bang! I learnt that he had Maltese heritage, and travelled there regularly to catch up with family although he lived in London, about 20 minutes from me. He was a widower, having lost his wife some ten years before. It's amazing how much you learn from passing strangers in a very short space of time; much more than you often do after spending months with people you know well, or work with every day.

All too soon the plane was landing and we had the usual routine of disembarking, *Sahha u Grazie* then passport control. We met up again by the carousel and he offered me a lift to my hotel while helping to retrieve my suitcase. I had already arranged transport so I had to decline, although I was dying to see more of him, in more ways than one.

As we exited customs, I noticed the board with my name on it from the waiting drivers. As soon as I said I was the expected passenger I was immediately whisked away to the waiting transport. There was no chance to say goodbye to Paul.

By six o'clock I had checked into the hotel, unpacked, showered, changed, found my way around and returned to my room to freshen up. Now I was ready to face the world. Descending down to dinner at seven I was a bit nervous, but soon realised that the predominantly English clientele included many people on their own, so I didn't feel out of place.

Even so, I didn't intend to spend my holiday with my own countrymen. After dinner I went for a walk to find the indigenous hotspots used by the locals. Taking a deep breath, I pushed open the door, walked up to the bar to order a drink and then lost my courage and tried to find a corner table to hide. There were no lonely tables and I soon found myself in conversation with various Maltese people who all asked personal questions without a trace of embarrassment. It was not what I was used to, but their friendly demeanour soon put me at ease. Questions that would have seemed intrusive and rude at home seemed natural here, and I gradually relaxed as I chatted with my new found friends.

Time flew past and it was gone two in the morning before I made my way back to my hotel room. Although I was a little tipsy after a full day and more than a few drinks, I realised this was probably one of the best decisions I had ever made. Forget being lonely; I had enjoyed more company and had more fun in the few hours I had been here than I had in many months. I woke the next morning with a smile on my face, the sun blazing through the open curtains of the balcony, and the confidence to face the world.

Digging out the skimpy bikini I thought I would never wear, I grabbed a towel, sun tan cream and headed for the beach. The weather was perfect; not so hot it was unbearable, but enough to make the cool of the water even more welcome. I was not looking my most sophisticated with the glow from the sun giving me the makings of a tan, my hair in rat's tails from swimming, and an old T-shirt and shorts thrown over my swimwear but I felt good.

It was typical that as I returned to the hotel, I saw Paul drinking coffee at a nearby bar, looking cool and striking in a pair of linen trousers and a striped top that showed off his biceps. He looked even more attractive than he had on the plane. After I had put my tongue back in, I was undecided whether to say "Hello," or run for cover. My dilemma was solved when he pulled out a chair and beckoned me over before calling a waiter and asking me if I wanted coffee or something stronger.

'Coffee would be fine,' I said as I settled myself, and tried to look glamorous despite the ravages of my day on the beach. As if to reassure me, he commented how lovely I looked with my sun kissed body, and didn't seem to notice my casual attire. We sat and talked for a while and he asked if I was spending my holiday on my own.

'Not all of it,' I explained. 'My friends are arriving tomorrow, but I caught an earlier flight.'

'What about tonight? If you haven't any other plans, it would be nice if you would let me take you to dinner.'

Before I knew it, I had a date to meet him at eight that evening. Skipping the meal provided by the hotel I spent hours getting ready and trying to decide what to wear. With my newly acquired tan I decided on a low-cut strapless dress and bolero. I realised I needed much less make-up than usual. Some dangly earrings, a simple cross and chain, and a dab of perfume completed my preparations. Grabbing my evening bag, I made my way down to the foyer just before eight.

He was already waiting in a chauffeur-driven car which took us to a beautiful open-air restaurant in a restored quarry some miles out. We ate, drank, dined and danced under the stairs until the car came to pick us up about one o'clock. The evening had flown, and although I had only met this guy less than thirty-six hours previously, I felt I had known him forever.

Against my better nature I was tempted to invite him back up to my room, but with a kiss that left my knees weak he said goodnight. No mention of seeing me again or arranging a further date. Oh well, it was good while it lasted and I would soon have the girl's company to keep me occupied. I spent the next day hanging around the pool, and was just dozing after lunch when I was pulled out of my reverie with screams and hugs from the girls who had just arrived.

'When did you get here? Look at you how brown you are. Why didn't you tell us you were coming?'

It felt good to be back with people I knew, but my thoughts kept returning to the man I had met so briefly and who had left me wanting more. That night was "Girl's night out" with a vengeance. We drank, danced and got down and dirty at the local night spot. We were constantly approached by various men trying to chat us up. I'm not surprised that with the noise we were making, and the amount we were drinking, they got the impression we were out on the pull.

A lot of flirting and teasing went on and they must have thought their luck was in, especially when we gave as good as we got by responding to their innuendos with 'If you're lucky,' and 'It's free at weekends.'

It was all in fun, the men were left disappointed, and around four a.m. the girls eventually made their drunken way back to their hotel rooms to sleep alone. One by one the girls emerged the following morning to take their places on sun loungers around the hotel pool. Peace reigned after the exuberance of the night before, with most of the girls reading or dozing in the wonderful sunshine.

Gradually the natural enthusiasm was restored, and by late afternoon the liveliness was back in the previously bloodshot eyes. Just before we all left to have a well-deserved siesta, a particularly fit young man came to clear away the sun loungers. As he was wearing very skimpy shorts, and with a hard-on to make the eyes water, the talk naturally reverted to the hot topic of sex.

'Would you?' Vicky asked with a nod towards him.

'Like a shot,' Mary replied instantly, 'although I would need a spray to get the cobwebs off first.'

The poor guy knew we were talking about him and blushed, even though his erection seemed to grow even bigger. Perhaps he liked older women and his fantasies matched ours. That night followed the formula of the previous one, although the men at this club were more mature, and a couple of the girls started to take them more seriously. In particular Liz, who had been single for more than a year since splitting with her partner, was attracted to a guy with a moustache who had been giving her the eye all evening.

We were not surprised when he asked her to dance to a particularly smoochy number, but at that moment there was a power cut and the lights went out. They came on a few minutes later, perhaps they had a backup generator, but we all noticed her dishevelled clothing and the embarrassed smiles. No one was surprised when about fifteen minutes later she made her excuses and left. We might have been Golden girls but when the time and opportunity coincided, we could still remember what it was all about. Around the pool the following morning she received the usual interrogation.

Her response was 'Well, the lights in the club went out and later in my apartment they stayed on, and 'Yes, yes, yes!'" Three times in one night, lucky girl.

Despite our brashness all the ladies with husbands, partners and significant others took it no further than mild philandering. The men in their lives will probably never realise it's not all about the sex. It was more about laughing, dancing, gossiping, flirting and being a woman instead of a housewife, mother and drudge. It was the feeling of knowing men still found you attractive, even if you were approaching bus pass age. It was getting a sun tan to overcome the winter blues, wearing clothes that look good on you on a Mediterranean island, that you would never dream of wearing in England. It was about being free and feeling happy and sexy. The holiday came to a close. We had memories, photos and promises for the next time.

As for me, well, I met up with Paul again several times after we returned home. We talked and got to know each other. He had my phone number and I had his. We kept in touch during the winter months, and arranged for him to spend Christmas and New Year with me in my new flat.

A touch of gold on the Christmas tree? Who knows?

I'd love to meet up with the Golden girls again next summer, but I have a feeling I might be otherwise engaged.

Honky Tonk Angel.

There have been many versions of this great country song, including one by Dolly Parton released in 1963.

I nearly didn't recognise her. Could this be the same plump little girl with fly-away hair who had followed me around like a puppy dog when we were growing up? She had been a sweet kid, but as a seventeen-year-old with raging hormones I didn't want a pre-teen cramping my style while I tried a new chat up line on an older woman.

'Hello, Max. Good to see you again. You've filled out a bit since the last time we met,' she said in a sultry voice that would melt diamonds.

'Do you two know each other?'

I recognised the older man possessively holding her arm as being one of the high flyers in the organisation; not someone to mess with.

'Good evening, Mr Lombardi. Yes, but it must be what, Suze, about fifteen years ago?'

'Something like that. And it's Suzanne now. You were probably the last one to ever call me Suze,' she smiled, with a sideways glance at her companion. 'Tony, shall we go on through?'

'Yes, of course, my dear. Nice to have met you Mr er..'

'Romano. Max Romano. Don't let me keep you Mr Lombardi. Have a nice evening.'

I noticed he bent close to her as they moved into the dining area, and guessed he was giving her the third degree. Better to keep out of their way for the rest of the evening. Not quite as easy as I hoped when the maître d' led me to a table only three away from where they were sitting. Although there were eight people on each table Suze was facing towards me, making it difficult to avoid her gaze. For a moment I saw the scared little girl behind the veneer of the sophisticated, expensively dressed woman dripping with sex appeal.

Although the food was excellent, and my business companions good company, I found it difficult to concentrate and was relieved when the band started up and conversation became more difficult. It was a private members club, exclusive and with an annual fee to make your eyes water. That's not to say it didn't have its sleazy side, which was the main reason I was there as part of an undercover investigation. The stakes were not about a few girls making money by providing personal services, it was much bigger than that. Money laundering on a scale to feed a minor African country for a year, people trafficking, drugs, you name it, and the prime suspect was the man leading my childhood friend into dinner.

Somehow I found it difficult to imagine Suze getting into something so obnoxious. Okay she hadn't had the easiest start, a father who was a drunkard and a mother who made money any way she could, but at heart I'd always believed she was a decent girl. Some of my family still lived close to hers, and over the years had kept me informed. I knew when her father died of alcohol poisoning, her mother married another deadbeat, and Suze had left home at sixteen amid rumours her stepfather had seen her as fair game. She had taken a job as a waitress in a Honky Tonk club fifty miles away, and was gradually building up a better life for herself. For a few years there was no more gossip, and although I never forgot her, I was concentrating on building up my own career.

Needing a cigarette break I excused myself and made my way to the conservatory designated as the smoking area. It had become such an anti-social habit I had the place to myself, but not for long.

'May I join you?'

'Of course,' I said, as she sat down next to me. 'We polluters have got to stick together.'

'Actually, I very rarely smoke these days. Just sometimes when it gets a bit much. Thanks. How have you been Max? Rumour has it you're working for the government. You seem to have done well for yourself. That suit and the Rolex didn't come out of a Christmas cracker.'

'I could say the same for you Suze,' I replied, not wanting to go into explanations about my job. 'You're looking good, but I'm not so sure about the company you're keeping. He wouldn't be my first choice of companion, or is it more than that? He looked very possessive of you.'

'He has his good side, but that's what I wanted to warn you about. You should leave. Now. He's had a tip off about you and ….What about old Mrs Jones and her chickens? Do you remember how she used to shout at us? Oh, hello Tony. Sorry. We were reminiscing about….'

'Perhaps it would be better if you returned to our table. Our guests were concerned you were unwell.'

'Yes, of course. Well, goodbye then Max. Take care.'

Why was she warning me off? It was more than just a jealous patron. Something must be going down tonight. I needed to get back to warn my associates. As I resumed my seat waiters came out of the woodwork, offering us brandies and checking our meal was satisfactory. It should have been good customer service, but my instincts told me it was more than that, as their constant presence made it impossible to have a private conversation. Five minutes later four gorillas took up positions near the door, confirming my suspicions.

'Perhaps it's time we called it a night?' I suggested, trying to give my team mates a hint.

'Unusual for you to be a party-pooper, Max,' one of the younger team members laughed. 'Normally it's us having to drag you away. The night's still young and I intend to make the most of it.'

Stupid idiot, why didn't he watch my body language? It was an important part of basic training.

'Anything wrong, Max?' The chief followed the direction of my eyes as I glanced towards the bouncers standing by the entrance. A frown crossed his face but he made no effort to move. 'Perhaps just extra security for pub kick-out time,' he said quietly.

Then all hell let loose. A woman screamed as a range of firepower appeared, and the goons made their way towards us. Without a second thought I upended the table, sending glasses and tableware crashing to the floor, but giving me a few vital seconds to dive towards the stage at the far end of the building. With the main exit blocked, I was banking on there being a back entrance somewhere behind the dressing rooms.

'Quick. This way.'

Just in time I recognised Suzanne's voice before self-preservation instincts had me opening fire with my own pistol. She dragged me into a small back room, used a key to open another door hidden behind a rack of costumes, and pushed me towards the iron staircase leading down from the fire exit.

'What about you? Come with me, you can't stay here.'

'No, Tony will get suspicious if I don't go back. Take care of yourself,' and with a quick kiss she went back the way we had come, and closed the door behind her. I heard the lock turn and had no choice but to flee down the steps and fetch help.

Despite being on high alert, it took fifteen long minutes before back-up arrived and forced their way into the club. What met us was a scene of devastation. From our party two were seriously injured, the youngster was dead, and only the chief had survived with just a few war-wounds. I was able to identify the goons, but Lombardi had disappeared.

'Check out the other rooms,' I yelled as I pushed aside the clothes rack to find my Honky Tonk Angel lying behind it in a bright red dress. Except her dress had been white until the gunshot wounds had changed its colour.

'You're safe,' she whispered. 'Good. Have a great life. Your angel will be watching over you.'

My promise to you, my sweet little friend. I'll find the man who gave you your wings and send him to the hell where he belongs. He will pay dearly.

Hush, not a word to Mary.

Another country style song, released by John Rowles in 1968. Although I knew the song, I'd never heard of the singer until a friend posted it on social media and inspired this story.

Jenny had been my best friend since our schooldays, but the past few weeks she seemed to have changed.

'Sorry, Mary. I'm too busy for coffee today. Perhaps in a week or so? Got to rush. Bye.'

It had become a tradition we would meet in the café in town every Thursday lunchtime to put the world to rights, but this was the third time she had made an excuse. Even stranger, was when I mentioned it to my husband John, he was reticent and tried to change the subject.

'Perhaps she's got things to do. You don't need to live in each other's pockets, even if you are friends. What's for dinner?'

He'd been acting oddly too, breaking off phone conversations when I came in the room, or changing his voice from whispered secrets to sounding as if he was giving instructions to one of his colleagues. We'd been childhood sweethearts and I believed we had a happy marriage. To celebrate our silver wedding anniversary, he'd surprised me with a cruise and we'd had a wonderful time, but now it seemed he had something on his mind.

'John, my birthday's at the end of the month, and I was wondering about booking somewhere for a nice meal. Half a century! Who'd believe it? What do you think? Or perhaps we could have a small party here, invite a few friends round?'

'You'd better count me out for that weekend,' he replied. 'There's a business trip coming up, and I might not be back in time. I'll bring in a bottle of wine, but it could be very late before I get home, especially if the plane's delayed. Leave it for now, perhaps we can do something the week after.'

Great. It looked as if I'd be spending the evening on my own, watching TV with a cup of cocoa. Now I really felt old. Well if that's the way it was, I'd make my own arrangements.

'Hi, Jen. What are you doing on the 29th? John's just told me he'll be away, so I thought we could go out somewhere for a meal to celebrate.'

'Oh. Hi Mary. Sorry, I'll be away that weekend. Another time perhaps.'

'Oh, OK. You didn't mention it before. Going anywhere nice? Have you got a new man on the scene you haven't told me about?'

Jenny had split with her husband ten years previously, and her disastrous marriage had made her somewhat wary of men. She'd been well rid of him; he'd been a drunkard and a bully, so it had taken a lot for her to start dating again. I'd been there to support her when she made the final break, and introduced her to one or two of John's friends.

'You're so lucky to have someone like John,' she'd told me at the time. 'Hard working, reliable and good looking too. Let me know if ever you get fed up with him.'

I'd laughed at the time, but now suspicion crept into my mind. Why hadn't she mentioned about being away? She knew when my birthday was, and had always been on hand to help me celebrate.

'Hello, Jen? You still there?' She hadn't answered my question. Perhaps she was trying to think up an excuse. I was sure I heard a man's voice in the background, and the phone sounded muffled, as if she was covering it with her hand. She knew I'd be pleased if she'd found someone, so why all the secrecy?

'Er, yes, sorry Mary. It's complicated. Look, I'll tell you more next month. See you.'

With that the phone went dead. Well blow her, then, if that's how she felt. I had other friends. Calls to Sue and Jackie produced the same result; everyone seemed to have picked that Saturday to have something better to do. John was quiet during the weekend, and I wasn't brave enough to have it out with him. Perhaps I was just feeling hurt, and letting my imagination run away with me. I knew he had to spend a few days in the North of England from Monday, for some important meetings. When he got back we could have a proper talk, he'd cuddle me and put my mind at rest, so it wasn't fair to upset him when he had a lot on his mind. I'd always trusted him before; why should this time be any different? And if there was a problem between us, well, I'd worry about that when the time came.

With the house empty it was a good excuse to do some spring cleaning. By Tuesday the kitchen was gleaming, with every single cupboard emptied, the contents sorted, rearranged and replaced, and I felt satisfaction at a job well done. Wednesday I went through the wardrobes and had two big bags ready to take to the charity shop. Thursday morning, I tried Jen's mobile but it went straight to voicemail, so either she was avoiding me or out somewhere with her new man. After delivering to the charity shop, I popped into the supermarket for a few bits, then, feeling hungry, decided to treat myself to lunch out. It was a beautiful day so I decided to go to a pub I rarely visited, and sit in the garden rather than the usual café. Placing my order at the bar, I went outside and selected one of the small booths, as although the sun was shining, there was still a chilly wind. The food was good, and with nothing to rush home for, I was enjoying reading my book when passing voices disturbed me. Peering out I recognised John and Jenny, deep in conversation. They both had their backs to me, and obviously hadn't noticed me hidden away, but were close enough for me to hear their voices.

'OK, that's all sorted then. I'll see you next week as arranged, but I think she's getting suspicious,' I heard John say.

'Hush, not a word to Mary,' Jenny answered. 'She'll find out soon enough. Take care, and I'll see you soon.' She gave him a hug before they went their separate ways, and I leaned back into the privacy of the corner. They'd always been affectionate with each other so why did this feel different? What were they doing meeting in secret?

Once the coast was clear, I headed home and was wallowing in the bath when I heard John's voice.

'It's only me, Mary. Are you upstairs? The meeting finished earlier than I expected, but I've already eaten so don't worry about dinner. I've got some work to do, so I'll be in the study for a while.'

'OK,' I called back, then decided to confront him. 'How was your meeting? What time did you get back? I thought I saw you in town lunchtime.'

'I didn't think you ever went to that pub,' he said, then realised his mistake. At that moment his mobile rang, and he grabbed at it as a life-saver, and started a long business discussion. 'Sorry, love,' he mouthed, 'I've got to take this.'

At least this time I knew he was telling the truth as I'd seen his boss's name come up on the screen. He was out most of the weekend, entertaining clients, or so he said, working long hours during the week, and off again early Thursday morning. When a huge bunch of flowers arrived from John on Saturday morning for my birthday, I was tempted to throw them in the bin. In the afternoon my sister phoned.

'Happy, birthday, Mary. Get your glad-rags on, we'll be picking you up at 7.'

'Thanks, Maggie, but to be honest I don't feel up to going out tonight.'

'Hush, Mary. Not a word, just be ready and wear something nice.'

I was tempted not to go, but in the end decided there was no point sitting around moping, and was ready and wearing my sexiest dress when she arrived in a cab.

'Where are we going? What's wrong with the car?' I asked.

'Wait and see, and nothing,' she answered, then refused to answer any questions until twenty minutes later we pulled into the impressive grounds of *The Grange*.

'This looks lovely,' I said. 'I've always wanted to go here. Pity John couldn't be with us,' then had to dive into the ladies before I disgraced myself by bursting into tears. When I emerged,

Maggie was nowhere in sight, but the reception desk directed me towards closed doors which appeared to lead to a room which was in darkness. Assuming there'd been a mistake, I turned just as the lights came on, a band struck up with "Happy Birthday," and I found myself facing a beautiful ballroom filled with my friends and family. At the front was John, with a grinning Jenny standing just behind him.

'We thought we'd been rumbled when we met last week to finalise the arrangements,' Jenny said. 'John wanted to tell you but I insisted it would be more fun if it was a surprise.'

'Happy birthday, darling,' John said as he led me onto the dance floor. 'It was difficult not to let it slip, but Jen kept nagging me, "Hush, not a word to Mary," so I hope it was worth it. Love you always.'

'You're forgiven,' I told him, knowing all my misgivings were unfounded.

I can't be with you tonight.

There's so much emotion is this song, released by Judy Boucher in 1986.

The text message came through as I was driving home from a shopping trip which had left my credit card glowing at the edges. Once I had pulled into our four-car garage, I checked my phone before going through to the house, a second sense warning me who had sent it.

'Darling. I know I said I wouldn't but I miss you so much. Can you get away the weekend after next? I've a business trip to Brighton on the 15th and will have a double room booked. Please say yes. Love you. X'

'Is that you, Judy?' my husband's voice drifted down the stairs.

'Yes. Be up in a minute,' I called back as I hastily deleted the message from my phone.

'Well. From the number of carrier bags, I'd say you had a successful day,' George said. 'Did you buy anything special?'

'Not really, but I did go a bit mad spending. I'm not safe to be left alone, sometimes.'

'As long as it makes you happy, Judy, you know I can afford it. Let me have the receipts tomorrow, and I'll get the accountant to clear them. Can't have you being stuck with no leeway on your card. Do you want me to increase the credit limit?'

'No, it's fine. You're too good to me as it is.'

'Darling. You know you're everything to me. By the way, did I tell you we've been invited to the Sanderson-Smythes for the weekend? I know you don't enjoy the shooting, but they do throw good parties, and they'll be several influential business prospects there, so I said we'd go.'

My heart sank but how could I refuse? Since the day we first met, George had been wonderful to me. My history with other men had been a total disaster. Somehow I had always attracted scumbags and lowlifes, and had been at my wit's end when he had come to my rescue like a knight in shining armour. Although he was thirty years my senior, he was a sweet, gentle man and I loved him like a favourite uncle. I knew he loved me in a similar way, and when he asked me to marry him it wasn't a great hardship to say yes. He needed a trophy wife, and I valued him as a friend and companion.

When we made love for the first time on our honeymoon, I realised how much of a struggle it was for him, and it suited us both to have a platonic relationship. I was still comparatively young and missed sex, but in many ways the affection made up for it, and having separate rooms gave me privacy when the needs became overwhelming. I intended to stay true to my vows, then I met Mike and everything changed. George had always been good to his employees, but I knew he was considering Mike as a successor when he eventually retired.

'Darling, you were the perfect hostess last night. Everyone in the office was talking about the party, and singing your praises. It really helps staff morale but I couldn't do it without you. Did you have a good time?'

'It was fun, George, but it was you they wanted to get to know. They would love it if you joined in, rather than sit alone and pay the bill at the end of the night. You're a good dancer. Why didn't you ask some of the ladies who were on their own?'

'You're the only one I want to dance with, sweetheart; I'm too old for small talk. Thank you for keeping the side up, I love watching you dance and enjoy yourself. Goodnight, my love. I'm off to bed.'

As he hugged me and gave me a chaste goodnight kiss, my mind turned to the handsome stranger who had recently joined his team. Mike was aware I was the boss's wife and had acted with decorum, but that hadn't stopped the sparks flying between us. It would be an impossible situation but our paths continued to cross as he became George's right hand man. It was natural we spent a lot of time together, and I enjoyed having the company of someone my own age. For the first time in my life I knew the meaning of real love. I thought of Mike constantly, we shared secrets and the occasions when we met up changed from open and public to clandestine. Did George suspect? I don't know. A part of me thought he would understand as long as we were discreet. Another part thought it could destroy Mike's career and my marriage, which was why the text message had me in a dilemma.

'George, you remember Jane,' I said at breakfast the next morning. 'She's getting married soon and the girls are having a hen party next weekend but I told them I couldn't make it. You'd think they'd go somewhere more exciting than down by the coast. Most brides these days elect to go abroad to keep the scandal to a minimum.'

'Why can't you go?' George replied as he buttered his toast. 'I'll miss you but I could pay the expenses as a wedding present. Is it too late to change your mind? You deserve a break with the girls.'

Sometimes I wished the man I had married was a total shit. He was so understanding it made me feel even more guilty at deceiving him. In the end I told him her parents were paying for the hen night but if he was sure, I'd like to go. I sent a text to Mike and tried to calm my nerves as the day approached. It was a wonderful weekend, and the start of many more covert meetings. If George was suspicious he never showed it, although he was quieter than usual, and didn't look very well. Perhaps he was working too hard?

What began as a fling turned into a love affair, and Mike asked me to file for a divorce so we could have a proper relationship. I'd always wanted children and with time slipping away, I knew this would be my last chance. He had found a new job abroad and given in his notice, and I decided to leave George and go with him. We arranged I would tell George face to face when he returned from work Friday evening, then I would join Mike at the hotel near the airport, before we flew out together early the following morning. It didn't work out like that.

Thursday evening George complained of chest pains but told me he was just overtired and would be fine after a good night's sleep. He insisted on going to work Friday morning although he looked very ill. My bags were packed and ready, and I was waiting for him to come home when his secretary phoned. He had been taken to the hospital with a suspected heart attack, and it was 50/50 whether he would pull through. Had he known all along? Had the thought of my leaving brought on the attack? Riddled with guilt I knew what I had to do. The text I sent to Mike later that night was the hardest thing I had ever done.

'Please understand my situation. I love you, but I can't be with you tonight.'

George recovered but became an invalid. Mike had told me if I didn't turn up it would be finished between us, and true to his word I never heard from him again.

I'll meet you at midnight.

A popular song by Smokie, released in 1976. Who doesn't dream of romantic midnight meetings?

I had finally fled from an abusive relationship, and against my better judgement allowed some friends to drag me off to a New Year's Eve party at a hotel. My self-confidence was at rock bottom, and it was hard to keep a smile plastered on my face.

All I wanted to do was go home, change into my PJs and curl up with a good book and maybe a glass of wine, to welcome in the New Year with Jules Holland on TV. That was another thing; since my escape I had taken refuge in the bottle, and although everyone was entitled to the odd drink, the recycling box of empties outside my house was becoming embarrassing.

I'd become so used to being told I was useless, stupid, couldn't cook, was no good in bed and couldn't even keep a house clean that I had lost all faith in myself. The one thing I had always been grateful for was my singing voice, but if I hadn't been tipsy, I wouldn't have had the courage to get up on stage. The hired band hadn't turned up for their final set, and my friends pushed me into it as a favour to the guy responsible for the entertainment.

I was shaking as I wracked my brains to remember some songs, but did a few numbers and couldn't believe the applause and calls for encores. Obviously everyone was merry, otherwise I'm sure they wouldn't have been so supportive. Noticing the time, I decided to finish with an old favourite of mine "I'll meet you at midnight." I sang the song as the minutes ticked away towards the midnight hour. As I finished someone started the countdown, Big Ben chimed and total strangers kissed, and wished each other a Happy New Year. By one o'clock I was home alone with a nightcap, and by one thirty I was snoring.

The first of January is always a peculiar day; most places are closed; the revellers are sleeping off their hangovers and there's none of the excitement of Christmas. The only thing to look forward to was months of bad weather and anti-climax until Easter, when the world starts coming back to life.

As it was a day when very few people worked, I was surprised to receive a phone call from an agent saying he had heard me sing and thought I had great potential. He gave his name as Bob Williams and wanted to arrange a meeting, to see if I was interested in signing a contract for him to become my manager.

I thought it was a wind-up, and ran through the list of possible culprits who had given him my number. Perhaps I was still on a high from the applause I had received the previous night, perhaps I was tired of being alone, perhaps I had finally decided to start taking back control of my life.

Whatever the reason, I agreed to meet him in a local coffee bar for lunch. Even if no-one turned up at least it would save me cooking, and I was used to eating on my own. As I hovered in the doorway of the restaurant a waiter came forward, and after confirming my name led me to a table where Bob was already seated. I recognised him from the party, but had escaped before my matchmaking friends tried to introduce me.

'First, an apology,' he said. 'I pulled in a few favours to get your phone number. I hope you don't mind but I never got the chance to thank you for saving my reputation yesterday. Suffice it to say that group are no longer on my list. Oh, just to prove I'm genuine, I brought along a few things for you to look at.'

With that he passed me a file with newspapers cuttings, links to publicity and review pages, all sorts of information about him and the entertainment company he controlled. He interrupted my browsing to ask what wine I preferred, but I was so surprised at being consulted I just mumbled 'whatever you're having.' After all the booze I'd consumed the previous evening I should probably have stuck to a soft drink, but he didn't seem concerned.

Somehow I didn't feel rushed, and even when I peeked to see if he was getting bored I noticed he was sitting quietly, looking at the menu. When I had finished reading, he smiled, passed me his business card and suggested we eat before we started to discuss the contract.

At first I was shy, but he began telling me about some of the odd people he had met during his career, and soon had me laughing at his stories. He was such easy company I found myself divulging things I had never told anyone else; how as a kid I had entered and won various local talent competitions, and had dreams of becoming a famous singer when I grew up. I had started making a name for myself in the local clubs, but everything came to a halt soon after my seventeenth birthday.

When I had first met Ryan, he told me he was an entrepreneur with contacts in the showbiz world, and would manage my career and make me a star. He became my manager and took over control of my finances and my life. I was installed in a small flat, which I later discovered was paid for from my own earnings. Ryan had a key and would turn up unexpectedly, then disappear for days without a word. If I queried anything, he would just tell me to concentrate on singing and leave the rest to him. He took my innocence and then my self-esteem.

'I hardly see anything of you these days. When will you be back?' I ventured one Tuesday afternoon as he emerged from the shower, ready to go out. It was bad timing on my part as I knew he was hung-over from the session with the boys the previous evening.'

'You ungrateful bitch,' he screamed as he backhanded me across the face. 'I'm working my guts off while you swan around all day doing nothing. I'll pick you up at 7.30 on Saturday for the gig at the Blue Moon. Be ready. And get this place cleaned up you slovenly cow.'

The door slammed behind him as I picked up his clothes from the floor where he had dropped them, collected the empty bottles and cans strewn all over the living room, and then burst into tears. It was the first time he hit me but not the last.

That was my life for the next few years as I sank deeper into depression and his temper grew steadily worse. My only release was on stage when I sang my heart out before returning to my prison. If another man so much as glanced at me in the clubs, Ryan went into wild fits of jealousy so I learnt to keep my head down, and never engaged with the audience once I had finished my session.

One night Ryan totally lost control. As I left the stage an older man started chatting and congratulated me on my performance, just before Ryan came to claim me. He was seriously drunk and went berserk, but fortunately the bouncers intervened before he could do any serious damage. Previously he had ensured the blows didn't show, but this time he was prepared to give me a beating in public. I found out later the older man was the owner of the club; he filed charges and Ryan ended up with a two-year jail sentence. The harsh judgement was explained when it was discovered he was also dealing drugs, taking advantage of my gigs to expand his trade.

Life had turned full circle. Now I was back, older and wiser, listening to another entrepreneur offering to make me a star, and wondering if I had learnt anything from my past experiences or whether history would repeat itself.

Four years have passed since that New Year's Eve party where I first met Bob. I'm waiting in the wings, ready to go on stage, but this time it's in Las Vegas and I'm the star of the show. I make my entrance to thunderous applause. As the minutes tick away towards the New Year, I launch into the song that made me famous and finally brought me happiness.

'I'll meet you at midnight' I sing to the handsome man seated in the front row. Bob, my manager and now my husband, gives me a wink as we share a secret smile.

I'll remember you.

One of Elvis Presley's less well-known songs, but a personal favourite. Beautiful lyrics.

I'll remember the smell of grass and the scent of the flowers, long after the summer is gone.

I'll remember the aroma of Christmas, and needles from the fir tree, mixing with the brightly coloured wrapping paper strewn across the living room floor. Happy times when the family was together, sad times when there was an empty chair.

I'll remember my first childhood friends, and occasionally search for them on social media, wondering what they are doing now.

I'll remember a favourite book, the characters and the fantasy, even though thousands of other words have long since taken their place.

I'll remember a long-forgotten song; the first few notes recreating the scene, the people and the vibrancy of youth.

I'll remember the landmarks in history; the assassinations, the wars, the deaths, the discoveries, the births and the opening up of whole new fields of knowledge.

I'll remember dancing until exhausted, but then unable to resist dancing some more until the morning sun chased away the darkness, and it was time to go home.

Sitting on the bench I gaze around at the rows of headstones, each one someone's memories.

I look down at your name and the dates engraved on a piece of stone; my mind is full and my heart overflowing.

I'll remember you.

It must be love.

Probably the best know version of this song is the one by Madness, but it was originally written and released by Labi Siffre in 1971.

We began as acquaintances when he started a job in the office block where I worked. Apart from his employers, most of the businesses in the building had only a dozen or so employees, so we all knew each other. It became a tradition to meet up after work on the nearest Friday after pay-day. We had a laugh, a whinge about life in general, and our bosses in particular, even if some of them were brave enough to join us in the pub. There were more decisions made, and complaints overcome over a few drinks, than in the more formal employer/employee atmosphere.

Jack worked for one of the larger firms, in a high-pressurised environment where results and targets were everything, and his colleagues tended to look down on us lesser mortals. After recognising several of us when he was having a solitary drink, he began to turn up regularly for our monthly socials. We became friends, and fell into the habit of exchanging first weekly, then daily emails. We rarely saw each other at work, and the pub was not conducive to personal chat, but over the months we gradually revealed more to each other of our secrets, thoughts and dreams.

It was an odd sort of relationship, a cross between social media acquaintances we'd never met, and long-standing friends who we'd trust with our lives. We were there for each other in the bad times, offering comfort and support, and the first to hear each other's good news.

'Hey, guess what? Against all the odds we won that big contract. I was ready to give up but you were so encouraging, I didn't want you to think I was a failure. Thanks, Tina. I owe you big time. See you Friday week. The drinks are on me. X'

The email from Jack made me smile, but the kiss at the end was the first time he had indicated we might be more than associates. Then I realised I was over thinking; I regularly ended my emails to girlfriends the same way, so it was probably nothing more than a friendly greeting.

'Go you,' I replied immediately. 'Make sure your boss appreciates it was all due to your hard work. You'll need that bonus to pay for the drinks I intend to wring out of you at the pub. See you then. X'

Well, if he was comfortable with signing off with a kiss, I could do the same. At the end of the month I was looking forward to hearing more about his success, but as usual fate intervened. My own manager was abroad, chasing some potentially lucrative business, and had forgotten the difference in time zones until I reminded him when he phoned me.

'I'm so sorry, Tina, but I really do need those figures tonight. Can you get them over to me for my meeting tomorrow? I'll pay you overtime but it really is important and I know I can rely on you.'

It was emotional blackmail but he was a good boss, so it was late by the time I turned up at the pub. As usual it was busy, and the only available space being at the far end of the table, I had no opportunity to speak to Jack, who had been commandeered by an inebriated Liz.

'Hi, Honey. Sorry about last night, but Liz was out of it and I had to make sure she got home safely. Are you free this Friday? Perhaps we could have a drink, just the two of us, without the usual crowd. Let me know how you're fixed. X'

It was unusual to receive an email from Jack on a Saturday, but I had already arranged to go away for a hen party weekend, so had to decline his invitation.

'No problem. That's what friends are for. Hope Liz was OK but I can't make Friday. How about the following week? I could meet you then. X'

'So sorry, and thanks for understanding but unfortunately no can do. I'm away that week following up on the contract, and the following week will be a nightmare, so it looks like it's going to be the usual pay-day meet before I see you again. I'll get there early and save you a seat. X'

When I turned up the place was heaving as there was a band playing that night. I squeezed in next to Jack, and although I could feel the heat of his thighs against mine, we had no chance to talk as the sound was deafening. We continued to meet up regularly with the others every month, but somehow our one-to-ones seldom materialised. Sometimes it was me who had to cancel, sometimes him, sometimes work commitments. Was it fate conspiring against us? I really wanted to know him better but was unsure how he viewed me. Were we friends, colleagues, or was he thinking something more?

He was in my dreams, often in my daytime thoughts, and his emails always made me smile. I felt bereft if I didn't hear from him, but how well did I really know him? I learnt more from his messages than our face to face conversations when the world and his wife were listening. Amongst company all we could do was laugh and join in the general whinges about life. From what he had told me privately, I was able to pick up on his throw-away comments, and we learnt to say so much without words. Was it enough? Should I be looking elsewhere for my happy ever after, and merely accept him as a valued confidante, as I did with a select few girlfriends I had known for years? My previous boyfriends had all been lust at first sight, and he didn't fit the mould. That put him firmly in the friends rather than the lover category, and yet…..We carried on in the same distant but remote relationship for two years until I received the email which changed my life.

'Need to see you urgently. Can I come round to your place tonight? Sorry for the short notice, but if you're free I'll bring take-away, chocolate and wine. Bribery and corruption, I know, but please say yes. It's important. X'

'You know chocolate will sway my heart,' I replied immediately, 'how can I resist? About eight? Do you need my address and directions how to get here?'

'Darling, if I admit how long I've known it, you might not let me come. LoL from your devoted stalker. X'

Although he'd seen me in every imaginable bad hair day, for some reason I got myself in a tizz deciding what to wear for when he arrived. I dashed around cleaning up, put on my best vamp dress, changed my mind and had just changed into my favourite comfortable but sexy outfit when the bell rang, promptly at eight.

'Your order, lady,' he said, thrusting a dozen yellow roses into my hand. 'By the way, is a humble delivery boy allowed to tell you how gorgeous you look tonight?'

'Come in, you nutter, before the food gets cold,' I said, relieved that his usual sense of humour had broken my anticipated concerns about entertaining a stranger. 'Stop standing around like a spare part and open the wine while I put these in water.'

The evening was a mixture of fun, laughter, serious talk and revelations. It turned out he had been head-hunted and offered a year's contract for a job in Europe by a rival company.

'It's a fantastic opportunity, Tina,' he told me. 'Double my existing wages, all expenses paid, and a similar deal for the staff I select to come with me.'

'I feel a "but" coming on,' I replied, not sure whether to congratulate him, or admit how much I would miss him.

'The "but" is will you come with me? I know it's a lot to ask, but I couldn't be happy any other way.'

'Why me?' I asked, even as I knew my answer would be yes.

'Guess, it must be love,' he said as he folded me into his arms.

'What took you so long?' I smiled. 'When do we leave?'

Johnny remember me.

An oldie with a haunting background, released in 1961 by John Leyton.

He was my first love when I was sweet sixteen. My parents didn't approve of his black leather jacket and motorbike, but they didn't know him as I did. Under his long hair and bad-boy looks was a gentle, caring man who only showed his wild side when he saw injustice, or if anyone came between him and his beloved animals.

His father was a wife-beater who ran off with another woman when he was five years old. His mother couldn't cope and turned to drink to get her through the miserable days, so his childhood was not a happy one. He learnt to look after himself when a long succession of uncles found his presence interfered with their desires for the woman who was still beautiful, even when she became an alcoholic.

'Evie, can't you get rid of that brat for a while? I didn't come here to babysit. He gives me the creeps, always hanging around and watching us.'

'That's not fair, Jim. He's a good kid, really. You're only after one thing, but there'll be no fun and games for you until I've got a drink inside me. Johnny, why don't you go and play outside for a while. I'll call you when I've finished talking to Uncle Jim.'

'Funny sort of talking, and he's not my Uncle.'

'Move, kid, or I'll do some talking with the back of my hand. And don't cheek your mother.'

I first met Johnny some years later when, as usual, he'd had to make himself scarce while his mother entertained. He was in the woods tending the damaged leg of a fox, who despite being a wild animal had not been resisting his touch until she sensed my presence.

'The poor thing,' I said. 'She looks in a bad way. Do you think she'll survive?'

Johnny put his fingers to his lips to warn me not to speak, as he reassured the animal in a soft voice that I didn't mean her any harm. He wrapped the vixen in his leather jacket, then beckoned me to follow as he set off through the trees, until the rear of a small house came into view. I watched as he laid the animal gently inside a rustic hutch, hidden away in the undergrowth. The interior was covered with a nest of twigs and leaves over an old blanket, and contained bowls for water and food.

'I'll try to get her some chicken or something, but I doubt if Mum has got any food in the place,' he said as he slid the bolt on the door of the cage. 'There's plenty of fresh water so she should be safe enough in here for a few hours. It'll give her time to rest her leg for a bit, away from predators. I'm Johnny by the way.'

'Sandy,' I answered, 'although my family insist on calling me Sandra. I've just thought. Our butcher always has left-over scraps. We get some for the dogs, sometimes. If we hurry, he might still be open. It's his late night tonight.'

'I know the one you mean,' Johnny smiled, 'but he won't help if he knows I'm involved. We had a bit of a run-in and I'm not his favourite person. You go, and meet me back here.'

'I can't. If I don't get home soon my parents will be sending out a search party. Look, come with me but stay out of sight. I'll do the talking then pass anything he gives me over to you. OK?'

'Fine,' he said, 'and thanks, Sandy.'

It wasn't the most romantic of meetings, but I think that's when I fell in love with him. The following morning, I retraced my steps and was peering into the hutch when I heard his voice behind me.

'Hello again, Sandy. Our little friend is doing well, and I think it's time to let her go. She said to tell you thanks for the chicken, it was delicious.'

'You look rough,' I said without thinking. 'Don't tell me you've been here all night. How did you get your parents to agree?'

'Thanks for the compliment,' he smiled, the twinkle in his eyes taking the sting out of his words as he noticed my embarrassment. 'My dad has been long gone, and Mum was out with her

131

latest boyfriend, so no one noticed I wasn't around. She's probably sleeping it off now. I guess from your uniform you're on your way to school; you don't want to be late.'

'I leave after this term so it doesn't matter much. Can I watch while you let her go?'

'OK. Stand behind me and try not to make any noise. She's still a bit skittish with strangers and we don't want to frighten her.'

I waited as he undid the lock, then gently reached in to ruffle the vixen's fur. She snuggled against his arm, trusting him completely as he guided her through the door until, after one final caress, he set her on the path to freedom. Her leg looked strong and healthy as she sprinted off, but she stopped once she was under the cover of the trees to give him a quick glance, as if to say thank you.

'She doesn't look as if there was ever anything wrong,' I said as she vanished from view. 'You must have healing hands.'

'Your magic chicken helped,' Johnny smiled. 'How about letting me buy you a coffee tonight to show my gratitude?'

'Sure. About seven in the coffee bar in town?'

'I'll be there.'

We dated for six months until my parents found out, and tried to ban me from seeing him. By then I'd left school and was due to go to college for two years, so I insisted I was old enough to make my own decisions about boyfriends.

'He's not good enough for you, Sandra,' Mum said. 'You'll soon be mixing with decent young men and find someone more respectable. I'm sure after your first term you'll have forgotten all about him.'

'I won't, even if I don't see him for a while. We're meeting tonight, so it's my last chance to say goodbye before I leave. I won't be late.'

That night he didn't turn up for our usual date. We'd always arranged our meetings as we went along, and he'd never given me his phone number. He'd taken me for rides on his bike, we'd walked hand in hand through the countryside, shared kisses in the back row of the cinema, but had never taken it further.

I'd told him I was a virgin, and although he was often frustrated, he'd never tried to push me. Perhaps I had been naïve, and I wondered if he'd lost patience and moved on to someone more willing. There was only one way to find out. Plucking up my courage, I made my way towards the house in the woods, near where he had tended the vixen. Following the path round, I knocked on the front door. At first there was no answer, but eventually I heard voices, and an inebriated woman in a pink negligee looked me up and down as she swayed in the narrow passageway.

'Yes? Did you want something?' she slurred. 'I'm nentertaining a friend, so state your business or go.'

'Does Johnny live here?' I asked, although from his description I was fairly certain this was his mother.

'Johnny. My sweet baby boy. 'cept he's not a baby any more. He's all grown up. He should be here, looking after me, but he took off like his no-good father. Left me all alone. What could I do? I need a man to look after me. My baby should be here to take care of his Mama.'

Tears started rolling down her cheeks, making a mess of her heavy mascara and eye shadow, until a man's voice called down from what I assumed was the bedroom.

'Evie! Get your arse back up here. Whoever it is, get rid of them. I'm waiting.'

'Hold your horses,' she yelled back. 'I'm talking to my young lady visitor.'

As she turned back towards me, her face cleared and she seemed to recognise me.

'Hey. I know you. You're my Johnny's beau. I saw your photo in his wallet when I was borrowing some money. How is he? When's he coming back to see me? Tell him I miss him.'

'He didn't turn up. I thought you might know where he is. When did you last see him?' I asked, although in my heart I knew he had moved on, and it was likely we would never meet again.

I thought of him often in the years that followed, had a lot of fun, dated a few guys, almost got engaged but broke it off, moved to another town and worked hard in my chosen career. Occasionally, I took trips back home to see friends and family, and it was on one such visit I learnt Johnny's mother had died. The whole town was talking about it. According to the rumours, she'd been drunk as usual, and got into an argument with a guy in the bar. They'd thrown her out, she'd wandered off into the night, fallen into the stream and drowned. A sad ending to a sad life. As usual the gossips had a field day.

'What did you expect, the sort of life she led. Strange men in and out every night. No sign of that reprobate son of hers. I wonder if he's heard the news?'

'Who would tell him? Nobody knows where he's gone. He hasn't been seen for years.'

'Can't really blame him, though. She wasn't exactly Mother of the year. I wonder what he's up to?'

'Probably in jail somewhere. You know what they say about the apple never falling far from the tree.'

'Has no one seen him at all?' I asked my parents over supper that evening.

'You're not still thinking about him, are you?' Mum said. 'That must have been, what? nearly 10 years ago when you had that teenage crush?'

'Nine, but there's a reason I was asking. Has he never been back?'

'Not as far as we know. If I remember correctly, he took off about the same time you left home. We did wonder if you'd run off together, but we checked with the college and all was well. Why were you asking about him? Old time's sake?'

'No, just something to do with work,' I told her. 'What's for dinner? I miss your blackberry crumble.'

It was quite a coincidence the case I'd been given was centred around my old home town. Killing two birds with one stone, I was able to fit in a long overdue family visit while I was investigating further. Would I get away with claiming Mum's crumble on my expense account? The thought of the accountant's face made me smile, but for now I had something more serious to take up my time. The following morning, after spending a couple of hours on research and getting nowhere, I thought I might have more luck with the gossips.

Most had long memories but wicked tongues, and were only too pleased to slag off Johnny, but couldn't provide any new information. I struck lucky when I stopped for a coffee, and bumped into an old school friend who was visiting her grandmother for the day.

'Sandy. Over here,' the voice called as I looked round the crowded café for a spare table. 'I thought it was you. How are you? I hear you're a big-shot in the city these days.'

'Jackie. Hi. Good to see you again,' I said as I joined her. 'Part business, part duty or should I say pleasure, catching up with the folks. What have you been up to?'

We sat and chatted for a while, comparing notes on other friends until she mentioned Johnny.

'Did you hear Johnny's mother died? Not that she deserved the name the way she neglected him, but he's a lovely guy. I always wondered if we would have got together if he hadn't been so smitten with you. Do you still see him? He never mentions you but then he was always one for secrets.'

'Mentions? You mean you're....?'

'No, not like that. I'm happily married with two kids. You remember George? My little monsters are five and nearly seven, but we hear from Johnny a couple of times a year. He had a hard time when his mother threw him out, but he sounded more positive the last time we heard from him. I've got his address. Would you like it? He lives about ten miles away, and I'm sure he'd love to see you. Unless your husband would object.'

'No, I never married, and yes please, I'd definitely like to look him up while I'm down here.'

We talked for a while longer, then, with the piece of paper tucked safely in my purse, I set the Sat Nav and drove off to rekindle memories and finish the task at hand. It was only when the metallic voice informed me I was nearly at my destination, I realised he would probably be working at this time of day. The thought hadn't occurred to me before, but as I was so close, I parked the car and began checking door numbers.

Number 46, like the other houses in the row, had once been grand but now looked run-down and shabby. Next to the front door was a row of bells numbered 1 to 12 indicating the various apartments, but none had name tags. Just as I was wondering whether to press one at random, a young woman carrying a toddler opened the door, and pulled it shut behind her before noticing me hovering.

'Yes? Can I help you?'

'Oh yes, thank you,' I stuttered as I gazed at the little boy. 'I was looking for someone called Johnny. Would you happen to know which flat is his?'

'I should do,' she laughed, 'but he's not in at the moment. John, sweetie, don't put your sticky hands on the lady,' she said as she pulled the boy away from my jacket. That's when I realised he had many of Johnny's features. 'May I ask who you are?' she continued, looking at me curiously. 'We don't see many of his friends here, but he should be back soon.'

'He was an old school friend, but I haven't seen him for many years,' I told her. 'Could I leave you my card? Perhaps you could ask him to phone me when he gets home. I've some news to tell him but I don't want to hold you up if you're on your way out.'

Thrusting the card in her hand I turned away, surprised to feel a lump in my throat, and my eyes welling up. I should have guessed he would be married with a family. A lot of water had passed under the bridge since I'd had my teenage crush, but I'd never forgotten him. Would she pass on my message, or conveniently forget to mention my call? I know what I would do, but not everyone was as curious as me. If I didn't hear from him within 48 hours, I'd have to try another approach.

With my eyes blurred with tears, I didn't see the man with an old Labrador on a lead until I nearly collided with him.

'Hey, are you OK? You seem really upset.'

'Johnny! Remember me?'

'Sandy! I don't believe it. Of course I remember you. I think about you all the time. What are you doing round here? I never thought I'd see you again.'

'Actually, I came to see you. Jackie gave me your address. I hope you don't mind.'

'Of course not. I owe her and George a visit so I'd better take some flowers as a thank you. Look, we can't talk here. I only live around the corner. Come home for a coffee. We've a lot to catch up.'

I felt awkward but let him lead me back to the house, and waited in the living room while he settled the dog before returning with some hot drinks. My first task was to tell him about his mother's death. He looked sad for a moment and I knew he was remembering all the hard times when he was growing up.

'Yes, the funeral's on Thursday,' he said. 'I know it's a lot to ask but she didn't have any real friends. Would you come? It won't be anything fancy. I can't afford much but she was still my Mum, for all her faults.'

'That was the other thing,' I started, just as the door opened and the young boy I had seen earlier burst into the room.

'Uncle Johnny. Did you make Sandy all better? Did you bring him home? Can I see him? Where is he? Does he need a cuddle?'

'Almost, yes, yes, yes and yes,' Johnny laughed. 'He's in his bed in the kitchen, but be very gentle. He's still a bit woozy from the operation.'

'Hello again,' his mother said as the boy scampered off. 'I hope you don't object to having a dog named after you but Johnny insisted. I don't think I introduced myself properly. I'm Pam, Johnny's cousin, although everyone says my youngster is the spitting image of him. Must be something in the genes. Listen to me rabbiting on. I'll leave you two to talk, but I hope to see a lot more of you, Sandy. He's been on his own too long, and I'm a sucker for happy endings.'

The room seemed very quiet after she left us, then we both started speaking at once.

'You were always the only girl for me, Sandy, but when you left...'

144

'It's lovely to see you again, Johnny but actually I'm here on business. Your mother....'

We both laughed and the time rolled away as we caught up with the missing years. True to form Johnny had volunteered to assist at a vet's surgery, and although at first his main duties had been cleaning up, he had been able to indulge his love of animals. When the old man died, he had left Johnny the practice which had gained in reputation but not in money, as he would pay the expenses out of his own pocket rather than see an animal suffer.

On the other hand, I had become very successful in the business sense, being head-hunted and earning exorbitant salaries, but never with a sense of fulfilment. After setting up and running my own company, I had been approached by a major client to track down a beneficiary, and distribute a substantial legacy. Whether by luck or judgement, Johnny's mother had kept up the payment of the premiums for an accidental death policy on her own life. The insurance company

145

had paid up, and I watched Johnny's face as he registered the number of 0s on the cheque I handed him.

'I can't believe this, Sandy. It's more than enough to fund the animal rescue centre I've always dreamt of, but I need someone to run the business side. I don't suppose…No, sorry. It's too much to ask.'

'Funny you should say that, Johnny. I wasn't sure if you'd remember me, but this was the final loose end to tie up after I sold my business. I'm moving back to this area and have already put in an offer on a house with extensive grounds backing onto the woods. If you need a business partner, I'm your girl.'

'You'll always be my girl, Sandy,' he told me, giving me a smile which made my heart flip.

Johnny remembered me.

Juliet.

A lovely ballad by The Four Pennies, released in 1964.

'Good afternoon, Miss Wiltshire. Please take a seat and make yourself comfortable while I have a quick read of your file. I notice you prefer the title Miss, rather than Ms. Is that correct?'

'Yes, when I was young you were either Miss or Mrs so I stick to the traditional.'

'I take it you never married then.'

'That's correct.'

'If you don't mind me saying, that's quite unusual for a lady of your years. I assume you've dedicated your life to your career, rather than raising a family. It's a very impressive CV.'

'Thank you.'

'Would you care to tell us something about yourself?'

'What would you like to know?' came the rather stilted response.

The members of the interviewing panel exchanged looks before the older man sitting in the centre of the trio took over.

'If I may explain a little about us, Miss Wiltshire. The company was started by my grandfather and is still run by his descendants. Naturally the people we employ have the highest level of expertise, but we also like to think of our staff as family. I hope you will understand if our questions are therefore directed to you as a person, as much as to your professional abilities. Our work often involves last minute late nights to meet deadlines. Have you any dependents or other reasons why this might prove inconvenient to you?'

'That's not a problem. My parents died some years ago, and I haven't any pets to worry about, so I can be flexible with my hours.'

For the first time the female member of the interviewing panel spoke up.

'We normally use first names here, Miss Wiltshire. Do you mind if I call you Juliet?'

'No, that's fine,' the woman said with a glance at the first man who had spoken, before turning back to the lady who had asked the question.

'Thank you. I'm Elizabeth, usually known as Liz. The gentleman in the centre is George, my father-in-law, and that's Mike on the end.'

'I know,' Juliet said before hastily changing the subject. 'Is there anything in particular I can tell you?'

'Shall we start off with the run-of-the mill questions? Why are you leaving your current employment, and what do you think you can bring to the company?'

Juliet noticeably relaxed as she explained that having reached the top position in her present job, she was looking for something to stretch her abilities. Her enthusiasm showed, and the initial chilly atmosphere dissipated as she went into more detail about the achievements listed on her application.

'Thank you, Juliet. That's excellent. We have a few more people to see before we make our decision, but I can tell you now, you are on the short list. You'll hear from us within a few days,' George said as he opened the door to see her out.

'Thank you for seeing me, George. Liz, I think we could work well together, and I look forward to hearing from you,' Juliet replied, hoping the omission of the third name wasn't obvious. Perhaps Mike wouldn't remember her. Twenty years was a long time, and they had both been teenagers when they thought they were in love. She wondered if he had a wife. It was unjust that a woman changed her name, but a man kept his even when he married. There should be some way of telling from their title. She wanted this job, but how would she cope at Christmas parties when presumably other halves were invited as a matter of course? The only way she would find out was if she was selected.

'I don't know about you, but I think Juliet would be the perfect fit for the team,' George said once the door had closed behind her. 'She's superbly qualified, a pleasant personality and has some great ideas for moving the business forward. What do you think, Liz? Mike?'

'She's definitely head and shoulders above the others we've seen so far,' Liz replied. 'I like her. Mike? You haven't said much, but I feel you have some reservations.'

'On paper, she's perfect,' Mike replied, 'but I'm not sure if she's the right one. Perhaps we should be looking for someone younger.'

'Come on, Mike. She's about the same age as you. What's really worrying you?'

'I just think we should see the other candidates before making a decision.'

'Fair enough. There's another four due tomorrow, so we can decide then. See you in the morning.'

Mike was thoughtful as he drove home and returned to his empty flat for a solitary meal. Despite the number of years that had passed, the sight of his first love still stirred his heart. She had a few more wrinkles, and had put on a bit of weight, but it suited her. Did she recognise him? Why had she never married? Had she always intended to be successful in her career, and a husband would have been merely a hindrance? He would have supported her if that's what she really wanted, but it seemed she had never really loved him as he had loved her. Even after all this time, he could still remember the anguish he felt when she told him she was going to work abroad, and it would be their last time together. How ironic that she had left him with the greatest gift a woman could give a man, by surrendering her virginity before moving out of his life forever.

'Hi. I'm home,' Juliet called as she opened her front door.

'Hello, darling. How did it go?'

'It was a bit weird actually. The interview was fine, and I think I've got a good chance, but there's one thing which might go against me.'

'Do you mean your age? We've lived together for nearly eighteen years, but you still won't believe me when I say you only look thirty.'

'No, it's not that. Sue, do you remember when we first met, and I told you I'd been with a man?'

'Yes. You dumped him when you realised your true sexuality. You said he took it very badly, but what's that got to do with the job?'

'Mike's the MD of the company, and I never actually told him the real reason I was breaking up with him. He assumed I'd just found another man.'

'That could be awkward. Still, if you get the job you could always invite him to our wedding. You'll make a beautiful bride. I can't wait until we exchange our vows.'

Late departure.

I believe this story was inspired by events in the TV series, 'Tales of the Unexpected.' Minor personality traits can become irritating.

'You're ten minutes late,' my boss said as I walked in.

'I'm so sorry,' I apologised. 'All the trains were cancelled, and the roads were blocked because of the snow. The pavements were so icy I couldn't walk very fast.'

'I'm teasing you Emma. We've got nearly fifty staff here, and you're the third to arrive. Most of them live at lot closer than you; it must have taken you hours. Thanks for making the effort.'

So that was me, never late, always the early arrival.

I was looking forward to my first ever cruise, and had spent weeks checking and double checking to ensure there would be no mishaps. What if the flight was delayed? Presumably the ship wouldn't wait for just one or two passengers, and would sail without me.

What would I do if I was stranded in a foreign country with no accommodation booked? Should I try and get a flight straight home, or sort out a hotel for the night? Why was I worrying? Presumably there would be a courier in charge of things, but it might be worth finding out the usual procedure.

It wouldn't have been so bad if my boyfriend was flying with me, but he had dropped his bombshell just after I had confirmed my booking.

'Hi Emma. Bit of a change of plan I'm afraid. Sorry for the late notice but the lads are going on a stag weekend in Amsterdam and I don't want to miss it, so I won't be coming. Sure you'll have a great time on your own. Have fun.'

Typical! We had been dating on and off for a while, but his cavalier attitude and lack of any idea of time-keeping drove me crazy. It was the final straw, and when I returned home I decided I would break up with him. We could still be friends but nothing more. In a way it was fortunate we had intended to book single cabins, so he could sort out his own refund; that's if he had even intended to go in the first place.

On departure day I checked my passport and itinerary documents for the tenth time, then sat looking out the window waiting for the cab. It turned up even earlier than my early booking, and we made good progress to the airport. Heavy rain had cleared away the snow so the roads were clear, and only the slushy remnants in the passing fields showed any signs of the bad weather of a few weeks before. I checked in, and with three hours to kill went to find a coffee.

'Emma! Over here!'

I turned at the sound of my name to find several of Mike's friends seated round a large table drinking beers, even though it was not much after ten in the morning.

'What are you lot still doing here?' I asked as I joined them. 'Where's Mike? I thought he was going with you.'

156

'He is, but you know Mike, he'll be late for his own funeral. Just as well our plane was delayed. He phoned a while ago to say he was on his way. Thought he would have been here by now.'

He was interrupted by the announcement over the loudspeaker.

"Passengers booked on the delayed flight 846A to Amsterdam please report to Gate 6 where your aircraft will be departing shortly. We apologise for any inconvenience caused by the adverse weather conditions."

'That's us. Have a great trip. If you see Mike tell him where to go, if you haven't already. He shouldn't have let you down like that,' Dave said, giving me a quick peck on the cheek before hurrying after the others.

My flight left on time, and after an easy passage through customs I immediately saw the courier waiting to greet the cruise passengers. Ticking me off on her list I was directed to the coach waiting outside, and before I knew it was

157

being welcomed by the ship's staff, and shown to my cabin. It was luxurious, and contained an enormous double bed.

'I think there's been some mistake,' I ventured. 'I only booked a single.'

'Your booking was upgraded, Madam,' I was told. 'There's nothing extra to pay but I'm sure you'll be more comfortable here. Your luggage will be delivered shortly, we sail at five, and you will hear an announcement to report to the main reception area for our compulsory safety instruction. Meanwhile feel free to look round the ship, but if you need anything the call button is here by the bed, or you can ask any member of staff. Have a good trip.'

After he left, I went out onto the balcony and basked in the warmth of the early afternoon sun, such a change from the dismal weather at home. A few minutes later my suitcases arrived, and that was the start of the most brilliant holiday of my life. Several of the single passengers had been placed on the same dining table, we all hit it off immediately, and they made great company as we met up for the various excursions.

I'd been having too much fun to check my social media, so it wasn't until we were heading for home that I took out my laptop and signed in. The number of posts in my feed was unbelievable, and it took me a while to trace back to the early ones. It was only by chance I came across Dave's post and the reams of comments underneath.

"Can't believe we were only speaking to him just before it happened. R.I.P. Mike."

"Terrible. Feel guilty now we were enjoying ourselves in Amsterdam while he was lying in hospital."

"Anyone know how it happened?"

"Local paper reported he was speeding on the motorway, skidded on the wet road, and hit an artic head on."

"OMG. Terrible. RIP."

I went cold, and for a moment tried to convince myself they were talking about someone else. Later comments made it obvious it was my

Mike; someone even asked if I had been told, and another replied I was away on a cruise so might not know.

There could be no doubt. By the time I finished reading it was gone midnight so I went to bed, convinced I wouldn't sleep, but was dead to the world within minutes of my head touching the pillow. Icy fingers caressing my shoulder made me shiver.

'Sorry I'm late Em. It took me quite a while to catch up. It's not like I could drive here but I didn't want to let you down.'

It was Mike's voice.

'Shove over a bit. God I'm freezing. How do you like the suite? I arranged the upgrade so we could share it and be together. It was meant to be a surprise; you would come in and find me waiting. I never intended to go with the boys, but the direct flight from the other airport should have got me to the ship before you. Things went a bit wrong but I'm here now, and I promise I'll never leave you or be late again.'

The feel of cold arms wrapping round me jolted me awake. God, what a horrible dream. Shaking, I got up. That's when I saw one side of the bed was soaking wet, and streaked with car oil and slushy mud.

Little Sister.

Another Elvis song which I remember singing to my sibling.

'Oh, Mum. Do I have to? I don't want her hanging around when I meet my friends. They'll laugh at me.'

'I'm sorry, son, but I've got to go to work or we won't eat this week. It'll only be for a few hours, and I'll make it up to you when we get back on our feet. I promise.'

It hadn't been easy for Mum since Dad died, and I felt a bit guilty, but I was fifteen and interested in girls; grown-up ones, not five-year olds.

'Can we go to the park, Joe-Joe? I want to feed the ducks? The big one has some new babies. We can get some food. Please. I promise I'll be good.'

'My name is Joseph, Susan. You don't like it when I call you Sue-Sue.'

Her bottom lip quivered, and I felt mean. She was a good kid really, and I didn't like to see her upset.

'Oh, go on then. We can't have Mummy Duck going hungry, can we?'

The usual beaming smile returned to her face and she rushed over to give me a hug. If only it was as easy to make Bethany smile as it was the other two ladies in my life.

'But no doing handstands and showing your knickers. You're a big girl now,' I teased.

At least it made Mum laugh, which didn't happen very often these days. I noticed her mouthing "Thank you," as she turned away to hide her smile. I had the money from my Saturday job so I could afford some bird seed from the local pet shop. It wasn't as if we had any spare bread in the house, and I'd heard it wasn't good for ducks anyway.

'Come on then, little 'un. Get your coat and shoes on, or I'll go without you.'

'I should be back by six, Joe, and we'll have something nice for tea for a change,' Mum said. 'You deserve it. I really don't know what I'd do without you. Sorry about messing up your chances with your young lady. Invite her over one day, I'd like to meet her. Now I must dash. See you later. Love you.'

I knew Mum meant well but I'd seen Bethany's house. Her father was something big in the city and it was a mansion compared to this place. No way could I ever invite her to this tiny flat in a run-down tower block, where the lift never worked and most of our neighbours were layabouts at best, and drug addicts at worst. At least the park was only a few minutes away, so we could escape to get some fresh air. Sue had a wonderful time and even my friends took delight in seeing her enjoying nature. All except Bethany.

'My God. Can't your family even afford a nanny for the brat?' she sneered. 'Don't even bother to talk to me until you've grown into a man, not a baby-sitter.'

I could feel my face turning red as she flounced off, giggling with her friends.

'Bitch.'

I hadn't noticed Lily come up behind me, but even though she was usually quiet and shy, the look she gave Bethany would have made anyone think twice about taking her on.

'Don't take any notice of her, Joe. She's not worth it. Sue's a lovely little girl, and I admire you for helping your Mum. That makes you a real man in my book.'

Her words made me think, and I realised how shallow the girl I fancied seemed, compared to the mature compassion Lily had shown. The next few years were not easy, but rather than taking a dead-end job, she encouraged me to continue my studies and make something of myself. We became best friends and I summoned up the courage to take Lily to the flea pit where I still lived, and introduced her to Mum.

'Wow, Mrs H. I love this room,' were her first words. 'Did you do it all yourself? It's fantastic. My ambition is to be an interior designer. Could you give me some pointers?'

It was typical of Lily that she ignored the smelly corridors and dire location, and made me look at the room in a whole new light. It was true, Mum had a way of using simple touches to make something come to life, and the two women were soon as thick as thieves. Even when I went off to college, Mum's letters were full of what a lovely girl Lily was, and how she had taken over my baby-sitting duties when Mum had to go to work.

Years passed, I obtained a well-paid job and eventually was able to find a small but perfect three-bedroomed house to rent. It was a far cry from the hovel we had lived in, but only a few miles away in an up and coming area. Sue was now at university, Mum and Lily had gone into business together, and although they weren't making a fortune, their reputation was spreading. Things were on the up.

I played the field with girlfriends, and although some of them were great fun, none measured up to Lily. We started dating and eventually I realised she was the one for me, and asked her to marry me.

'It took you long enough,' was Mum's delighted response. 'Lily's always been like another daughter to me, and at least she knows what to expect from her future Mother-in-law. Congratulations to you both. Had you made any plans yet?'

'Hang on, Mum,' I said. 'We've only just got engaged but it'll probably be sometime this autumn.'

'As long as your little sister doesn't beat us to it,' Lily replied. 'I want her as my maid of honour.'

'What are you talking about?' I asked, puzzled 'Do you mean Sue? Fine if you want her as a bridesmaid, but she's still a kid, certainly not old enough to think about getting married herself.'

'It might have escaped your notice, but your little sister is now a beautiful woman,' Lily replied. 'She'll be twenty next month, and she's been seeing Jack for nearly two years. They're not rushing into anything until she's got her degree, but he's a lovely man and they're well suited.'

Our wedding day was magical, Lily looked stunning, and before our first wedding anniversary I was the proud father of gorgeous twin girls. What chance does a poor man have surrounded by all these females? As I wait to escort my little sister up the aisle, to give her away to the man she loves, I'm hoping she and Jack might produce some boys before I get totally outnumbered.

Love Story.

This story arose from a challenge to write a love story with a Happy Ever After which didn't end up being sloppy.

She had a cold. Her nose was red from constantly blowing it, her stomach was bloated from the curse and her hair was in dire need of a wash and cut. It was a wet, miserable night but having run out of coffee she had to make the late-night trip to the 24-hour supermarket. Perhaps while she was there, she could pick up a flu remedy.

Unfortunately they were stored on the top shelf and there was not an assistant in sight to bring one down for her. Her balance was off-synch, so it was not surprising that as she stretched to grab the packet the whole display came crashing down around her.

With her face now as red as her nose, she struggled to put them back into some semblance of order before anyone noticed. Mortified at her clumsiness she saw an arm reaching to help before she registered the gorgeous male to whom it belonged.

The second thing she noticed was the concern in his beautiful brown eyes as he asked if she was okay. Not only did he restore everything back to its proper place, he even carried her bags as he gently took her arm to lead her into the all-night coffee bar within the shopping complex.

As they sat and chatted, she realised this was the man she had been looking for all her life. Unbelievably he seemed to feel the same way about her. It was love at first sight. They dated, got engaged and her wedding day was the happiest of her life.

In their luxury honeymoon suite, she smiled as she remembered their first meeting. He was in the bathroom brushing his teeth as they prepared for their first night of wedded bliss. It was something to tell their grandchildren in the years to come.

****

It was as he slipped between the sheets next to her, that she first noticed his extended canines.

Well, what did you expect?

Making up for lost time.

If you've ever caught up with a long-lost love from your youth, this story might be particularly poignant.

'Jenny? Jenny Blackwater? I can't believe it. Is it really you?'

'Arthur Tompkins, as I live and breathe. You haven't changed a bit. And it's Jenny Ferguson now. You must remember Jack; we would have been married 30 years this year.'

'So you're a widow now. When did you lose him?'

'Five years ago, last Christmas. What about you? I remember you were sweet on Betty at one time.'

'Betty was a lovely girl, but there was only ever one for me, and Jack won her heart.'

'Mr Arthur Tompkins, please. Hello Mr Tompkins. We're ready for you now. Will you follow me?'

'Jenny. I shouldn't be very long. Will you wait for me? We can have a coffee or something and catch up on old times.'

'That would be lovely Arthur. I think I'm next so I'll meet you back here.'

Half an hour later they were seated at a table drinking coffee, and it was as if the intervening years had never happened.

'How did you get on? What did they say, if you don't mind me asking?'

'Great. The bone has healed up perfectly, and I can't say I'm sorry to see the back of that plaster-cast. I'll take more care in future when I decide to trip over steps. That was six weeks out of my life. How about you?'

'I've got about six weeks as well.'

'I didn't notice any plaster, Arthur. Is it your leg?'

'No, nothing broken except me. The cancer has spread and there's nothing else they can do. It's a lot to ask Jenny, but would you keep me company for my last few weeks? Just for old times' sake.'

Malta is a woman.

Many years ago, a Maltese man told me the story of how he emigrated to Australia, but was pulled back to his tiny homeland to spend his final years. It inspired me to write this poem, dedicated to "Aussie Mike."

This island is a woman
surrounded by the sea,
but how can she still claim me?
Why won't she set me free?

I left her for a new world,
a vast, exciting land.
I sailed across two oceans
to free her wedding band.

And in this new existence,
I made a brand-new start,
I found someone who loved me
and gave to her my heart.

175

For a few years we were happy,
my prospects all seemed bright.
We worked hard in the daytime,
and loved away the night.

But jealousy beset her,
the land that was my home,
she wanted me a prisoner,
she would not let me roam.

Her claim could not be broken,
she crept into my mind,
and once a woman has been scorned
she never will be kind.

And soon she pulled me home again,
now I'm a prisoner here,
my love I left behind me,
each day I pass in fear.

For though the chains of love are strong,
in my heart I know,

the sea around my island

will never let me go.

Message to Martha.

A lovely song, released by Adam Faith in 1964 was the inspiration for this story.

Martha was a sweet girl, but a bit too staid and respectable for me. There were plenty of other girls around, ready and willing to share the wild life I craved. I knew she had a crush on me, but I wasn't the type to spend my Sundays listening to the church choir. She did have a good voice though, and I enjoyed accompanying her on my guitar but insisted she sing rock, rather than dreary ballads or romantic rubbish.

Deciding there was nothing for me in this little hick town, I took off for the big city to find an agent for my band. Bob and Mitch were happy to come along, but not so keen when I suggested we have Martha join the band.

'Little Miss Goody two-shoes? You must be joking,' Mitch said. 'You gonna rename us "The girl guides" or something?'

'Yeah,' Dave chipped in, 'just as well I'm not coming with you. I'm not shaving my hairy legs for any female.'

'If you'd stayed with us, Dave,' I told him, 'we wouldn't be looking for another singer. I can handle the vocals. You stay here and waste your life, but don't come begging when I'm rich and famous, and you're still panicking how you're going to pay the next bill.'

As it happened, Bob's girl got pregnant and he decided to stay behind and support her. When he heard the news, Mitch changed his mind about coming, so I was on my own. They probably did me a favour; I'd have more chance without those deadbeats holding me back. Martha and I would have made a great duo, but for one thing her parents wouldn't allow it, and she insisted she needed to finish her exams first.

'You know I'd love to come, Zak, but it's almost impossible to make a living in a band. At least if I had some other qualifications to fall back on, I could get a job and carry on singing as a hobby at the weekends.'

'Please yourself, but don't say I didn't give you the opportunity,' I replied. Although I had guessed what her answer would be, I was still disappointed. The first few years were tough, dossing in flea-bitten hotels as I travelled all over the country for small-time gigs in pubs and clubs, but gradually things improved and I built up a good reputation. Still, it would have been no life for a lady in those early days.

Eventually, I got myself an agent, and the money became more regular and the venues better. Although not rich, I started thinking of buying a place to settle down. The strain of being constantly on the road was beginning to show, and I wasn't getting any younger. Brian was a decent guy, and although he took his 20%, his expertise saved me being ripped off on several occasions and he earned his cut. The only thing we disagreed on was my style.

'You're not a kid anymore, Zak, and Rock and Roll isn't in favour these days; you need to move with the times. You've got the voice and should consider a more cabaret style. That's where the future lies. Ditch the leathers, get a tux, learn some ballads or easy listening and you'll never be out of work. You can throw the odd rock song into the act, but don't make it all you do. Diversify and I can get you plenty of bookings. Stay as you are, and it's not worth my time. All I ask is you give it some thought.'

It was a hard decision to make as Rock and Roll was my life, but I swallowed my pride and my career took off. I became an "A-lister" and instead of begging for work, Brian was able to pick and choose which engagements we would accept, and negotiate bigger and better fees. Perhaps I wanted to show off and prove how successful I had become, but for the greatest show of my life I sent a message to Martha, including a best-seat ticket, and invited her to join me as my guest. I was delighted when she accepted. On the night, I was more nervous about seeing her again, than I was about facing a crowd of thousands of adoring fans. The show was a fantastic success, but I had given my all and was totally drained when Brian came into my dressing room.

'Lady to see you, Zak,' he said. 'One of your biggest fans.'

'Brian, you know my rules by now. I need some peace, a few drinks, and to discuss how it went before I face the public. Let me unwind a bit and invite whoever it is to the after-show party. For now, I need some space.'

'Hello, Zak. Sorry, I didn't mean to intrude. I'll catch you later.'

It took me a moment to register that the gorgeous female standing in the doorway was my old childhood friend.

'Martha! You don't count. I mean, come in,' I stuttered like a schoolboy as I felt myself blushing at my crass remark. 'You're a friend not a fan. It's wonderful to see you. How have you been? Are you still singing your Holey, Moley stuff?'

Talk about both feet first but she smiled as she took a seat in the crowded room.

'Thank you, you too, great, not exactly and you were fantastic. I'm so pleased you achieved your dreams,' she laughed as she answered my barrage of questions.

We only had a short while to chat before I had to go to the party, and although I encouraged her to come, she said she had an early start the following morning, so wouldn't be able to stay. When I looked for her later, Brian told me she had already left. I realised nearly all our earlier conversations had been about me; she was such a good listener, but I felt bad I hadn't asked if she was still singing, or what she was doing now. Over the next few months I had no time to think about anything except the next record, the next sell-out tour. When I had a moment, I would send a message to Martha, but they tended to be about my latest success and never about her. She always replied, but only once did she mention she had a performance of her own coming up at a famous venue, and how excited she was.

'I must remember to ask her all about it,' I thought, but the following week I was off on tour again, and the message never got sent. On the way back to the hotel in the early hours of the morning, after another exhausting but sell-out show, I was dozing in the back of the limousine when a screech brought me wide-awake. The next thing I knew the car was turning somersaults, and I blacked out.

'Nurse, I think he's coming round.' A quiet voice I recognised drifted into the fog of my brain.

'About time too,' someone responded. 'I'll call the doctor.'

'Martha. What are you doing here? What happened?' I asked as I recognised her standing by my bedside.

'You were in an accident. I was on my way to do the show in Vegas when I got your message, so came straight here instead.'

'Vegas? Why didn't you tell me? I'm fine, go and catch your plane.'

'Zak, you've been out of it for ten days. They'll be other opportunities for me, but I couldn't leave while you were in a coma. It was odd about the message, though. When I looked for it again, I couldn't find it. Perhaps it got deleted, but it served its purpose and told me where to find you.'

A shiver went up my spine at the thought of all she had given up for me.

'Martha, I never sent any message.'

My Little friend.

A sweet song by Elvis was the inspiration for this story, but the ending might be a surprise.

'Hey, Mike. Don't look now but I think your little friend is following you.'

'Oh, not again. Come on guys. I'll race you to the stream.'

Pedalling as fast as I could, she was soon left far behind as the others grabbed their bikes and pelted after me. She was a sweet kid really, but it was embarrassing the way she followed me about. Why couldn't she find some girls of her own age to play with? She was a skinny little thing and the boys in our gang could be a bit rough. Several times I'd had to stick up for her, which gave them even more reason to tease me. I was big and strong for my age, so they didn't push me too far, but she was always referred to as "My little friend."

My family weren't well off, but we lived in a decent house, were well fed and clothed, and Christmas and birthdays always brought a generous present. She lived with her Mum in a slum shack in the woods, had never known her father, and was usually dressed in clothes either miles too big or too small. We went to the same school, but as she was five years younger than me, I only saw her at breaks, standing alone and forlorn in a corner of the playground. The other girls her age seemed to ignore her, but although kids can be cruel, it wasn't my problem.

'Dinner's nearly ready, Mike. Get washed up then go and sit with your gran until I call you. It's your favourite tonight, steak pie.'

'OK, thanks Mum,' I said as I wandered into the front room to talk to my grandmother. Although she was old, and had to use a stick to get around, Gran did talk a lot of sense, so I enjoyed chatting to her. She could be quite harsh at times, but she also spoilt me occasionally, slipping me some money behind Mum and Dad's backs, and winking to tell me to keep it a secret.

'Hello, Mike. What have you been up to today? You look as if you've been dragged through a hedge backwards. It's a good job those jeans are hard-wearing, but they could do with a good wash. I suppose you've been playing down by the stream.'

'Hi, Gran. Yes, I slipped in the mud, but these are my old ones, so it doesn't matter.'

'I saw you rush off when your little friend turned up. Poor child. She idolises you, you know.'

'It's so embarrassing, Gran. She's always trailing round after me. She's not big enough to keep up with us, and anyway, she's a girl.'

'You might look on girls differently in a few years' time, lad,' Gran laughed, 'but it's always good to be kind. If you can stand up for someone weaker than you now, it'll put you in good stead for when you're a man.'

I never forgot her words, but soon after moved to a senior school so very rarely saw Sally. I only found out her name because the family mentioned her now and then, and sometimes Mum made me take some food to her house, pretending she'd made too much. Sally's mother was an old witch, and although I wasn't frightened of her, I hated going there. What with my little friend mooning around after me, and her mother stinking of booze, I escaped as quickly as I could. The years passed and eventually I went off to college, and learnt what Gran meant when she said about looking at girls in a different way. I dated, got drunk, went a bit wild, studied hard and returned as a man.

'Hello, Mike. Welcome home, and congratulations on your degree. I always knew you had a decent brain somewhere inside that woolly head of yours,' Gran said as she wrapped me into a hug. 'Look who's here. You won't mind sleeping on the camp bed for a few days, will you? Sally's staying for a little while, so we gave her your room as you were away.'

'Hello, Mike. Good to see you again, but I don't want to put you out. I'll go home tonight, Mrs Perkins. It'll be fine now, I'm sure.'

'Nonsense, young lady,' Gran replied. 'You stay here until it's sorted. Now sit down, Mike and tell us what you've been up to.'

Sally had grown up in the years I'd been away, but I noticed her eyes still followed me as they had when we were kids. After everyone had gone to bed, Gran came to sit next to me on the settee.

'Thank you for giving up your bed, Michael. That house wasn't safe for a young girl like that, even if she does know how to look after herself.'

'What happened, Gran? I noticed the bruises on her face.'

'It's been going on for a while, but it all came to a head last week. Her Mother's fancy man has been knocking her about, but it seems he noticed she was growing into a woman, and tried to take advantage.'

'Poor kid. Is she alright? Did they catch him?'

'Apparently, she kicked him in his crown jewels, and he took off after giving her those bruises. The police haven't caught him yet, so she came to us for help. You don't mind about giving up your room?'

'Of course not. She can stay as long as she likes. Let's hope the law catches up with him before I do.'

He was never caught, a few more years passed. I found a job and flat in the city, and only went home every couple of months. The family kept me up to date with news of my little friend, who had now grown into a beautiful woman. Her mother had died as an alcoholic, and with support from my parents she had managed to evict her mother's latest boyfriend, and was now living in the hut on her own.

'We're a bit worried about her actually,' Mum told me on one of my visits. 'There's rumours that bloke has been around again, perhaps seeing if her mother left anything worth having.'

'Do you want me to pop over?' I asked.

'Yes, I'm sure she's fine but she'd be delighted to see you. It's been a while since you were home.'

It was nearly dark as I set off across the woods, and I wondered how she felt as a woman on her own, stuck right out here. I hoped I wouldn't frighten her knocking on the door so late. As I approached the shack, I heard the sound of raised voices, and rushing up the path through the trees, could see the shadow of a man trying to force his way through the open front door.

'I'm not a little girl, anymore,' I heard Sally scream. 'Now get out of here before I give you another kick where it hurts the most.'

'Not this time, lady,' a drunken voice slurred. 'This time I'm gonna finish what I started all those years ago.'

My rugby tackle sent him flying to the ground, and a couple of punches knocked him out cold.

'Are you OK, Sally?' I asked as she fell into my arms.

'Do you realise that's the first time you've called me by name, Mike?' she sobbed. 'Your parents said you were home so when I heard someone at the door, I assumed it was you. Sorry to drag you into this mess. I always cause you problems.'

'Hey, it's not your fault. I take it that was the scumbag who attacked you when your Mum was alive. You'd better call the police to come and get him before I forget myself.'

'My hero. You've always been there for me since we were kids. Even when I drove you mad mooning around after you. Don't try and deny it. I know I was a pest but things are different now.'

That was a year ago. Now I'm standing in the church porch, waiting for the bride to arrive. I feel nervous, but probably not as nervous as my best friend, Jake. It was me who introduced them, so I was delighted when Sally asked me to give her away. My little friend had found the man of her dreams, but will always have a special place in my heart, even if she was never the girl for me.

193

Not Fade away.

A great Rolling Stones song, and one of the greatest forms of true love.

Today was one of her good days. Underneath her frail body the beautiful girl of my dreams still resided.

'Do you fancy a cup of tea, Grace? It's a lovely day. We could sit out on the patio if you like.'

'Thanks, Brian. That would be lovely. Can you bring it out when you've made it? I'm still a bit slow so I'll start making my way now. Two sugars, and cake would be nice.'

Her radiant smile still lightened my heart, and the fact she was getting her appetite back was encouraging. She'd never been fat, but her once robust figure was now almost scrawny, and the clothes hung off her emaciated frame.

'OK, but be careful. You're still very weak and some of those flagstones are a bit uneven. I don't want you falling.'

'Stop flapping, man and just do as you're told.'

The words sounded harsh, but she was laughing as she said them and I was happy to oblige. Keeping half an eye on the kettle I watched her rise carefully from the armchair, and make her way to the rocking chair before collapsing into it with a quiet sigh. However much she tried to hide it, I knew the effort it took to walk even that short distance. The sun felt warm as I placed the tray gently on the table next to her, unsure if she was dozing as she sat with her eyes closed, an open book resting on her lap. For a while she didn't stir and I was able to study her unobserved.

Her skin was still smooth, but seemed thinner somehow, and several bruises were visible on her arms and legs. Her newly washed hair glistened in the sunlight, which caught the grey streaks threaded between the mass of jet black which she'd always tended with such care. Now it showed some straggly ends and was in need of a good cut. Would a trip to the hairdressers be too much for her? Perhaps I could find one who would come and do it at home.

'What are you looking at?'

Her voice interrupted my thoughts although her eyes remained partially closed.

'No gentleman would figuratively strip a lady with such an intrusive examination.'

'Sorry, darling, but you're still beautiful, and no man could resist gazing at you. How are you feeling? Would you be up to it if I could find someone to give you a trim?'

'First he flatters me, then he implies I look a mess,' she said as she ran her hand through her hair. 'You're right, though, it definitely needs doing but I haven't had the energy before. I wonder if anyone does home visits?'

'That's exactly what I was thinking; I'll have a look later. Here's your tea. Is it warm enough? I'll make some fresh if you like.'

'No, it's fine, except it's very sweet. Did you put sugar in it?'

'Yes, two spoonful's as you asked.'

'But you know I don't take sugar. You've been making my tea for years so you should have learnt by now. Did you find the biscuits?'

'I thought you wanted cake. Shall I go and find some?'

'No, cake will be fine. I tell you what, let's forget the tea and have a glass of wine. The sun must be over the yardarm somewhere. I wonder where that expression came from? I'm so forgetful these days.'

'It's not surprising with all you've been through. You were always so active, it must have been hell doing nothing all those weeks in hospital, but at least you're home now. I'll go and see what we've got.'

As I rummaged through the sideboard for the Christmas left-overs, I wondered if I was losing my marbles. I knew she didn't usually take sugar, but had assumed she asked for some as an energy boost, or perhaps I had got it wrong. Discovering an unopened bottle of Chardonnay, I picked it up, found two glasses and the corkscrew, and took them into the garden.

'Would Modom like to taste the wine?' I asked, flourishing the dishcloth like a waiter. 'It's a cheeky little number, grown on the south side of the allotment with just a hint of smelly socks. Shall I pour?'

'I thought you were making tea,' she replied as I opened the bottle. 'Never mind, it's nearly five so let's be decadent. Did I tell you I bumped into Father yesterday? Well, I didn't actually speak to him, but I saw him when I was walking along the cliff top. I called out but he didn't hear me.'

'Whose father? Do you mean the priest? Your father died nearly twenty years ago.'

'I know that, you daft lump. Did I say Father? I haven't been to church in years. Old Father Jack must be retired by now. I bet the new man is all modern and doesn't say mass in Latin. It's probably all Hallelujahs and happy, clappy. Still, I would quite like to go one Sunday. Would you take me?'

'Of course, sweetheart. Whenever you feel up to it. Cheers.'

'Cheers. Ooh, this is nice. I hope you're not trying to get me drunk so you can take advantage of me, you wicked man.'

The memories of that lovely evening helped to sustain me in the weeks that followed. It was the last night I spent with the woman I loved before the terrible disease reclaimed her, and I became a stranger she didn't even recognise. As I stand here by her grave with a bunch of her favourite flowers, I remember the woman I lost twice. Which was the hardest? I hope even in her darkest times she understood my love for her would never fade away.

Perfect Day.

Something we all need occasionally, this song was written and released by Lou Reed in 1972. It was subsequently re-released as a Charity single.

I met her when I tripped over my own feet, and succeeded in throwing a sticky concoction of fruit juices all over her pristine white sundress.

'I'm so sorry. Look what I've done. I'll pay for it to be cleaned. Do you want to take it off? I mean, not now of course, later. No, I don't mean that. I mean. Oh God. I'm so sorry. What can I do to help?'

She sat up in shock from the chair where she'd been relaxing, and stared in horror at the orange and mauve splodges. My stuttered apologies hadn't helped, and my ineffective attempts using my handkerchief to clean the marks had only made them worse. I'd even managed to get some in her beautiful blonde hair, and the book she'd been reading was now a tacky, crumpled mess. As she took off her sunglasses to survey the damage properly, I was mesmerised by her piercing blue eyes, which in other circumstances would have turned any man to jelly.

The silence stretched between us as she blinked in the morning sun, and then she laughed.

'You don't do things by half, do you?' she said as she looked at me properly. 'If you wanted an introduction, you only had to ask. Usually men have a more subtle way of chatting me up. It's Sara, and the book wasn't very good anyway.'

'Mark,' I replied, holding out my hand in greeting.

'Nice to meet you, Mark,' she said, 'but forgive me if I don't shake hands.'

Following her glance, I looked at my tacky fingers and watched as the last few drops from the glass dripped onto her bare legs.

'I'd better leave you before I cause any more damage,' I said. 'Look, I'm in room 203. Get the hotel to launder everything, and tell them to put it on my bill. I'm really sorry.'

With that I scuttled back to my room to clean myself up. In other circumstances I would have asked her out, but I didn't think she'd want to spend time with me after I'd been so clumsy. Although it was gone mid-day, the other guys had only just emerged after a heavy session the previous evening. They were congregated at the beach bar, and already downing beers as if they were going out of fashion. I enjoyed a drink, but what should have been an interesting holiday was turning into a booze cruise, and I half regretted agreeing to join them. It had been a last-minute decision when someone dropped out, but getting paralytic every day was not my idea of fun.

'There's a coach trip this afternoon to see some of the local sights,' I told them. 'Anyone fancy joining me?'

'Nah, mate. Being herded about's not my idea of a good time. It's your round.'

I paid for the beers, but then decided I didn't want to spend the afternoon drinking. We'd hardly ventured outside the confines of the hotel, and the brochure I'd seen looked interesting. Heading for reception, I managed to book the last remaining place, and after a quick change from my swimming gear, was just in time to catch the coach before it pulled off. It was packed, and my numbered ticket was right at the back in the only remaining seat.

'Hello, again. At least if you're stalking me there's no sticky drinks this time.'

It was her.

'I'm not. Honestly. There was only one place left. I didn't realise it would be next to you,' I stuttered like a tongue-tied schoolboy, instead of a mature man of twenty-nine. At that moment the coach lurched, and I was thrown across her lap.

'You'd better sit down before you cause any more damage,' she smiled. 'I was only teasing but you are a bit of a disaster area.'

Thankfully there were no more mishaps, and we spent the afternoon together getting to know each other. I learnt she was twenty-six, had recently broken up with her boyfriend, and had decided to book a last-minute holiday to get away from the repercussions.

'It wasn't until I broke it off that I realised how much he was a control freak,' she told me. 'Everything had to be his way, and we actually had very little in common. The final straw was when he informed me we were spending our holiday on his parent's farm in the wilds of nowhere. I love animals, but wanted a bit of sun, sand and pampering, not mucking out in muddy fields. We argued, and here I am. What about you?'

I told her about the pub arranging the trip, and how I wanted to see some of the local culture, but the others weren't interested.

'This is more my sort of thing,' I said. 'That museum showing how they used to live and work was fascinating, and I like this traditional village. I'm glad I came, especially as you're sharing it with me. That café looks quaint. Do you fancy a coffee?'

'Only if it's not self-service' she said with a grin. 'I didn't bring a change of clothes with me.'

By the time the coach dropped us back at the hotel, it was as if we'd known each other for ever, and I was totally smitten. It was a perfect day, and I'd fallen in love. She agreed to meet me that evening, and we dined and danced under the stars in a romantic open-air night-club. The rest of the holiday passed all too quickly as we spent every minute together.

'We'll keep in touch,' I told her on our last night. 'It's only a hundred miles or so. I can come down to you at weekends, or you can come up to London. And in between there's always Skype or Facetime. We'll make it work somehow. What do you think?'

'I'd like to, but I've some things to sort out first. I don't want it to be on the rebound, or just a holiday romance. Things can look different when it's back to reality. Let's see how it goes.'

That was nearly two years ago, but I haven't forgotten that perfect day. I've even arranged for a glass of sticky fruit juice to be included with the champagne at the reception. As the wedding march struck up, I turned to see my beautiful blonde, blue-eyed bride walking up the aisle towards me.

Today will be an even more perfect day.

Race with the Devil.

Versions of this song title were released by Gene Vincent in 1956, and by Gun twelve years later. It was also an action horror film.

'He's a good lad really, even if he is a bit of a devil sometimes.'

'You're too soft on him, Mary. You know what they say about spare the rod.'

As usual the vicious old woman next door was slagging me off and stirring up trouble. If I was a devil, her tongue was pure evil. For all her holier than thou demeanour she delighted in gossiping about the younger generation, and if there was nothing to say, she'd make something up. It wasn't the first time we'd had a run-in, and after I punched her son on the nose, she went out of her way to make life difficult for me.

Gregory was a nasty little weasel, and just because the family were well off, thought he was better than the rest of us. For his 21st birthday, darling Greg had been given a flash sports car. My

Mother had bought me a second-hand headlight for the motorbike I was building, but I know which gift was most appreciated. Since Dad ran off when I was a toddler, she had brought me up on her own, and worked two or three jobs to keep food on the table and a roof over our heads. I was proud of her, and determined to win the prize money in the big race to buy her something nice, as a way of showing my gratitude.

I didn't have a girlfriend, but if I did it would have been someone like Jenny. She was a pretty girl, quiet and shy, studying hard to be a vet. That didn't stop Gregory constantly pestering her for a date, but when she made it clear she wasn't interested, he and his mother joined forces to spread rumours about her being easy with her favours. It wasn't fair, but it wasn't my business although I did feel sorry for her.

Exceeding the speed limit was wrong, but the tranquil, country roads were far out of town, and I wanted to open the bike up to see what it could do. Well pleased with the result, I'd slowed down to check I hadn't pushed too far when I heard a disturbance from the nearby trees.

'Please, stop it. You said you'd help with my car. If you can't get it going, just let me phone the garage.'

'It's much more fun to play. Come on, you know you want to.'

'Stop it, Greg. Leave me alone or I'll scream.'

'No one will hear you way out here, and even if they did, I'd tell them you led me on.'

It was Jenny's voice, and she sounded really scared. Pushing through the trees I confronted the bully as I tried to keep my temper under control.

'I can hear you, Greg. The lady said leave her alone. Now move away, and let her be.'

'Look who it is! Mr bad boy himself. What makes you think they'd take your word over mine? You call that a lady? You're welcome to her.'

That's when I punched him. He wasn't man enough to stay and fight but took off in his flash car, dripping blood from his nose all over his shiny new leather seats. I managed to get Jenny's car started then followed her on the bike until she was safely home. I didn't see her after that, but Gregory soon had the rumour mill working overtime, telling everyone he had tried to rescue the girl when I attacked him. That, together with my customary outfit of black leathers, soon earned me the nickname of "Devil," while Greg's white car and round, chubby face had him designated as the "Angel."

The competition organisers had a field day with publicity for *"Race with the Devil,"* but all the betting was on the Angel beating me in the race. I wondered how much it would cost his family to cajole, blackmail or bribe the judges, but was determined to win fair and square. Jenny had stopped attending college, and hadn't turned up for her regular work experience with the local vet. It seemed the tittle-tattle had hit her hard, and I heard on the grapevine she had moved to another town, unable to face the shame of being labelled as a cheap slut.

Once I had some money in my pocket, it might be worth trying to find her, and let her know most people knew Greg for a liar and a cheat, but were too weak to stand up to him and his family in her defence. For now, the important thing was the race. Although we were a small town, it had become a major event and entries came from miles around. The starting line was in the fields behind the square, then along the main road leading out of town, up the hill, through the twisting country lanes, along the dirt track by the quarry, then back in a loop for the home stretch. The race was unusual in that bikes and cars competed against each other, although most of the entrants were Greg's cronies, which would ensure he won.

Not this time. There were very few bikes apart from mine, which I had built from scratch and finished off with a black and red devil painted on the fuel tank. It was a bright, sunny afternoon as we lined up for the start. Greg's car was in the centre, and the other cars were tightly packed around him, leaving the only space at the outermost point. I realised that was the reason the judges had stopped me entering the field until the cars had taken their places, so I would have the worst position.

With a loud bang, the starter gun fired and we were off. The white Angel sped into the lead as I was forced to hold back behind a solid mass of cars, which were going deliberately slowly to block me. After a few miles the pack opened up as some dropped out, and the narrow lanes gave me an advantage. Weaving in and out I opened up the throttle, and in the distance caught sight of Greg's car entering the stretch by the quarry. 80, 90, 100. I broke the ton as I pounded along the dirt track, steadily gaining on the white angel. By the time he heard me, no other competitors were in sight, and even the supporters had opted for the comfort of the finish line with its fairground atmosphere. It was just him and me.

Inch by inch I narrowed the gap. The wind whistled through the thick trees on one side, and emerged to escape over the sheer drop into the quarry as I seized my chance to overtake him. Sheer adrenalin kept my wheels grounded as I pulled alongside ready to move into the lead. The sneer on his face was the last thing I saw as he wrenched the steering wheel hard to the left, sending me spinning into nothingness.

'I'm sorry, Mum. I tried,' I said, as the rocky ground sped up to meet me.

Was I hallucinating? The white of Greg's car as it crashed far below and exploded into flames was not the only White Angel around that day. Feathery white wings surrounded Jenny's angelic face as I felt myself lifted until I opened my eyes to see the bike sprawled a few feet away from where I lay on the path.

The rescue party discovered not only Greg's charred remains by his burnt-out car, but Jenny's body buried in the undergrowth nearby. She had been dead a week. The inquest opened tongues, and once all the facts were revealed it was generally accepted that Greg had murdered Jenny, and hidden her body near the spot where he had died.

The race with the Devil had ended with the true Angel taking her revenge.

Save the last dance for me.

I've written two very different stories inspired by this song title- this is one of them. The song was released by The Drifters in 1960.

We met when she was 15 and I was 19. Teenagers with raging hormones, but despite the ribbing from my friends I instinctively knew Rose was the girl for me. We dated for a while, lived, loved and laughed, then went our separate ways in the big, wide world.

Although I often thought of her, my work took me all over the country, and it was a few years before I saw her again. She had remained friends with my sister, who kept me updated on who she was seeing, and what she was doing.

'*Hi Jim.*' Sally's email hit my personal inbox while I was finishing off a contract in New York. '*Just to let you know the party's been organised for my birthday. Obviously you'll be aware of the date, but knowing what big brothers are like, it's the 25th. Get your penguin suit ready, it's going to*

215

be posh! At The Grange, no less. Dinner at 7.30 and carriages at midnight, so no pulling a Cinderella act and turning up late. Hire a helicopter if you must, but be there! And don't forget I want a BIG, expensive present. Rose has split with that toe-rag she was seeing so you can be her "plus one." See you on the 25th. If you've got anything else arranged, cancel it! Love Sal. X'

I couldn't believe my baby sister would soon be 21, but that meant Rose must be a similar age as they'd been in the same class at school. It would be good to see her again. Well, both of them, obviously. Sally could be a pain, but she was family, whereas Rose was, and always would be, special. I was looking forward to spending the evening with her, but things didn't work out quite as planned. Knowing the timing would be tight, I'd booked an overnight stay at the hotel, and arranged for a taxi to take me there direct from the airport. At least I'd be on the spot if we were held up by traffic, and would have time to freshen up while everyone else was enjoying their first course.

"We regret to announce that due to the adverse weather conditions, the 5.35 a.m. flight to London is experiencing delays. We apologise for the inconvenience and will keep you informed. Please listen out for further announcements."

Great. I'd pulled out all the stops to finish the project so I would be in time for the party, and now it looked as if I'd not only be late, but shattered from lack of sleep and sitting around at airports waiting for the fog to clear. Sally wasn't best pleased when I sent her a message explaining, but what could I do? It was impossible to concentrate as the hours crept past and the departure board remained blank, but just as I was on the point of giving up, the tannoy announced the boarding gate and I was finally on my way.

Thankfully, there were no hold-ups at Heathrow when the plane landed, and I promised the taxi I would pay any fines and double his fare if he put his foot down. Despite his best efforts it was already 11.35 p.m. when we pulled into the parking area at The Grange. After checking in and the quickest shower ever, by the time I had thrown on my monkey suit and found the ballroom it was nearly midnight.

'Ladies and gentlemen. It's been a wonderful evening and our hostess, Sally has asked me to thank you all for coming, and for the wonderful gifts. This will be a birthday to remember. Please take your partners for the final dance of the evening, that old favourite, "Save the last dance for me." On behalf of the band, I would like to wish you Goodnight and a safe journey home.'

I couldn't see my sister amongst the crowd, but the smile Rose gave me as I held out my hand to invite her to dance was worth every hassle of the day. We didn't have much chance to talk, but I held her close, she put her head on my shoulder, and I stole a quick kiss before she was whisked away as the evening ended.

'It was lovely to see you again, Jim,' she said, 'even if it was very short and sweet. Thanks for the dance.'

'I'm sorry it wasn't longer, Rose,' I told her. 'It's been one of those days, but I'll keep in touch. Perhaps we can meet up one night, and make time for more than just the last dance. See you soon.'

Again, fate intervened. The following day, after catching up with some sleep, I was enjoying a leisurely lunch and checking my phone when an urgent message popped up from the MD of the company I had been working for.

'Need you here, like yesterday. Phone me as soon as you see this. Damn time zones.'

By early evening I was winging my way back to the states, with no opportunity to arrange a proper date with Rose. The problems had been nothing to do with my work, and it seemed the main man had been so impressed he immediately signed me up for a lucrative, extended contract. It was another two years before I returned to the UK, and I assumed my lovely girl would have given up waiting for me.

It all seems like yesterday, but the memories are as fresh and new as they were fifty years ago.

Our family and great grandchildren encourage us as we take to the dance floor to celebrate our golden anniversary. Temporarily discarding our walking sticks, we hang on to each other for mutual support as the band strikes up, and as usual, my darling Rose has saved the last dance for me.

Take me with you.

The melancholy of leaving behind the sunshine after a holiday, and a 'What if' scenario combined to be the inspiration for this story.

It was a typical gloomy, depressing day in London; hard to believe that only 24 hours previously I had been basking in the warmth of the Mediterranean with the temperature over 30 degrees. As I headed through town it started to drizzle, so naturally every cab driver decided to go into hiding, the buses were full to bursting with tourists, and there were the usual delays on the tube.

By the time I reached my office I was soaked to the skin and in a foul mood, which didn't improve when I found my assistant had phoned in sick that morning, and my partner had been called away urgently to sort out a major problem.

Internet connection had been poor whilst I was abroad, but I hadn't expected to face over nine hundred e-mails as soon as I switched on my

221

computer. Add to the mix a temp who was worse than useless, and my being the only one with any authority to give instructions and handle complaints, and the day went from bad to worse. By three o'clock my stomach was protesting and my brain felt ready to explode.

'I'm going out. I'll be back later,' I shouted as I headed for the local sandwich bar to escape. To get some peace, I had deliberately left my mobile on the desk, but after eating a calorie laden lunch and starting to feel more human, I took out my iPad to browse through some photos of happier times.

One in particular brought a smile to my face. I had been on a tour visiting ancient monuments, and had wandered off by myself to discover more of the surrounding area when I stumbled across a stone-clad cottage. The door opened to my touch, and feeling rather guilty I stepped inside to shelter from the burning sun. It was difficult to tell if it was inhabited as although beds, chairs, tables and cabinets were all still in place, everything was covered by thick layers of spiders' webs.

I couldn't resist taking a few pictures until, hearing a noise behind me, I turned suddenly to catch a glimpse of a beautiful woman in her late twenties, dressed in what I could only describe as 60s hippy style. Unusually for the locals she was blonde with very pale skin, and not the olive colouring of the local villagers.

'I'm so sorry; I didn't mean to startle you. Is this your home? It was very rude of me to intrude without permission, please forgive me.'

'I'm lonely, stay for a while,' came the whispered response.

'Oh, you speak English. What's your name?'

'I was named Ambrosine, although my friends called me Zena. By what name are you known?'

'Anthony, but my friends call me Tony. Do you live here alone?'

'The others have moved on, but I am trapped until I can find someone to rescue me.'

'Rescue you from what, or who? Why don't you just leave if you want to?'

'You don't understand. Until someone agrees to accompany me, I am doomed to stay forever in this place. Where do you live?'

'In a city in England. It's cold, rainy, overcrowded and miserable; not like this beautiful area with the sunshine and trees.'

'Take me with you.'

'Where? Back to London? Do you have a passport?'

'You will be my passport, as I will be yours,' she answered.

It was a weird sort of conversation, and it crossed my mind the sun might have addled my brain, or perhaps she was simple and this was where she came to hide.

'Tony. Tony. Are you there?'

The voice from outside calling my name made me jump, and when I turned, she was gone.

'I'm in here,' I called.

'Where? I can't see you. The coach is leaving soon. It's a long walk back if you miss it.'

'OK. I'm coming,' I said, although I would have preferred to examine the others rooms to say goodbye to Zena first, but I didn't want to keep my companions waiting.

'Where did you spring from?' Paul asked as I closed the door behind me and moved towards him.

'I was in the cottage. It was odd....'

'What cottage? Come on, we'd better hurry up.'

The rest of the week was the usual drinking, eating and doing what young men on holiday always do. After a particularly heavy session the previous evening, most of the gang were content to hang around in the hotel, but I wanted some space so decided to make one last visit to see if I could find the cottage again. The area looked familiar, but at first all I could see was hilly mounds and undergrowth. Just as I thought it must be the wrong place, I caught a glimpse of the sun reflecting on the honey coloured stones and there it was. The undergrowth seemed thicker but the door opened to my touch, and Zena greeted me with a beaming smile.

'Tony, you came back for me.'

'I'm sorry I didn't say goodbye before. We go home tomorrow, so I can't stay long.'

'You have your passport? Show me, please.'

I didn't usually carry it around, but had put it in my pocket so I wouldn't forget it when we flew home the following day. Even as I took it out to show her, I wondered if it was a wise decision. It could be part of an identity theft trap, involving police reports and delays catching my flight. I needn't have worried. All she did was stroke the photo and hand it straight back to me. As I put it away, I thought I caught a glimpse of two photos on the page, but that was ridiculous.

'I must go, now. It was lovely to meet you. Take care of yourself, Zena.'

'Thank you, Tony for rescuing me,' she said. 'We will be happy,' then she kissed my cheek and I was alone.

The only other peculiar event was when I was going through passport control.

'Collective passports are no longer valid, Sir. Your spouse must have her own.'

'Sorry? What are you talking about?'

'My apologies. It must have been the light. I thought I saw two photos.'

Realising how time had slipped away while I had been indulging in holiday memories, I went back to work to try and catch up. By eight that evening I decided enough was enough, packed up and went home. As I opened my front door, I was aware of an enticing smell coming from the kitchen. I lived on my own and my evening meal was usually a take-away, but this reminded me of fresh food and continental cooking.

'Hello, Tony. Thank you again for helping me escape. You must be tired. I'll make you a drink then serve up your dinner. You relax. I'm here now to help you as you helped me. We will be so happy together.'

I thought I had been dreaming, until I woke the following morning to find a soft body cuddled up next to me.

The psychiatric doctor had been making copious notes as I told my story, and I saw the words 'stress, work pressures, holiday?' written on his notepad. Why could no one else see her? She's real. I know she's real.

Valentine's day.

Who can remember waiting for the postman to deliver that very special Valentine's day card, and trying to work out who sent it?

14 days to go

Fourteen days until all the cards come flooding through the door and the florist delivers a beautiful bouquet. The postman thinks what an attractive, popular young girl I must be, instead of a middle-aged woman with a birthday.

13 days to go

Twenty years ago, I would have received at least two Valentine's cards; one from the current beau and the other from my mum, to save face in case I didn't get any others!

12 days to go

Another wild, abandoned, hectic weekend over. Well, at least I had a nice meal with the girls on Saturday night. I could almost convince myself the guitarist in the restaurant was giving me the eye. Almost but not quite, as he was doing the same to every other female in the place. Still, at least I can pretend I'm not past it.

11 days to go

A surprisingly good day at work. The sun even managed to shine a bit and cheer up the everlasting winter. The train actually turned up on time, I got a seat and Peter was in a good mood for a change. I think it's something to do with his new girlfriend. He thinks it's an office secret. He should know by now the most efficient thing in the office is the grapevine.

It's his own fault really, If I was trying to keep something quiet, I wouldn't meet for lunch in the wine bar just around the corner from the office. What does he expect so soon after pay day? That everyone is going to have a yoghurt at their desk? They save that for the broke days at the end of the month.

Actually his girlfriend seemed very nice. Although she had a stunning figure, beautiful face and a radiant smile she appeared friendly and normal. She even smiled at Lucy from the office, when she was trying to be 006 and trailing the boss and his paramour without being detected.

Her secret squirrel activities remind me of the guy who used to work with us. What was his name? Jack? No James. That was it. Everyone called him Jimbo. He left the firm to start up his own detective agency. It must have been two or three years ago.

Now *his* girlfriend at the time was a class A bitch. She had expensive clothes, family with pots of money and claws worse than any big cat in a zoo. I never could see understand what he saw in her. He was such a nice guy, pleasant to everyone and good looking too.

I remember the time Maggie was so upset when her dog died. Some of the younger ones were taking the mick but he took the trouble to listen to her. It was Jimbo who found out that her husband had given her the puppy on their wedding day, only two years before he was killed in a car accident. He couldn't have been more than thirty something.

231

The look on Maggie's face when she received a dozen red roses on Valentine's day. Everyone was teasing her about her secret admirer but she always denied knowing who sent them. It's only just occurred to me. I bet it was Jimbo. It's just the sort of thoughtful thing he would do to help cheer someone up.

10 days to go.

Making up for yesterday; sleety rain, train cancelled. Probably due to "people on the platform." I'm sure it would run perfectly to time if no one wanted to catch it. Peter in a foul mood; perhaps his girlfriend realised she could do better than him.

Maureen has invited me to a dinner party on Saturday night. I'm not sure if I'll go. I know she means well but I do get fed up with her constant match-making. It wouldn't be so bad if the spare men she seems to know were not Adonis-looking, but they always seem to be boring and drippy. Surely there must be some interesting, unmarried men over thirty left in this big, wide world who don't look like the back of a bus.

Check what's on the telly this Saturday. Great; football, a war film or a documentary about antiques. I'm beginning to feel like an antique myself. "Middle-aged." What a horrible expression. If the life span is three score years and ten, I suppose theoretically I am half way through.

Psychologically I'm in the prime of life- young enough to enjoy myself and old enough to have enough money to do it. No responsibilities. I should be having a whale of a time, instead of tossing up between a boring dinner party and dozing off in front of the box with a glass of wine on a Saturday night. What's on at the pictures? "Bambi," another war film or "Young Emmanuelle."

Fantastic. The last one will be full of yobs trying to show how macho they are, or old men trying to remember what to do. Right. Maureen's it is then.

9 days to go

Life goes on.

8 days to go

What am I going to do on my birthday? I could ask the girls to join me for a meal somewhere but I bet everywhere is booked up now. Anyway, all the restaurants would be full of young couples gazing like dopes into each other's eyes, or maybe arguing because he didn't send her a sloppy card. That's the trouble with being born so close to Valentine's day.

7 days to go

Saturday night. Perhaps I should splash out and buy a fabulous, sexy new outfit for tonight, and knock 'em dead. Why bother? The old faithful "little black dress" will do.

Sunday 1 p.m.

Unbelievable. I'd just been thinking about Jimbo after all this time and who was the spare man at Maureen's last night? Got it in one! He was every bit as nice as I remembered him and even better looking. Within five minutes we were chatting again like old friends. When Maureen made it obvious we were keeping her from her beauty sleep, we shared a cab home. He gave me a goodnight kiss as he dropped me off but refused my offer of coffee as it was so late. Although he didn't ask for my phone number he promised to keep in touch. The bimbo is off the scene- I hope he phones.

Monday

He didn't phone.

Tuesday

Peter nearly had kittens as I was so long on the phone. Who cares? I had forgotten Jim would have the old work number and I'm meeting him tomorrow night.

Wednesday

How can time go so slowly, one hundred and fifty minutes to go. I hope he turns up.

Thursday

Brilliant evening. I feel sixteen again. He is so nice. Roll on tomorrow.

Friday- late

Another great evening. Must get some sleep to look good for my birthday tomorrow. (I mean today.) Jim is taking me out somewhere special to celebrate. Why did he ask if my passport was up to date?

Saturday- *The day*

Two cards! A dozen yellow roses for my birthday, a dozen red roses for "A very special lady." Dinner in Paris with a fantastic man. What more could a girl want? Thank you, my patron Saint Valentine. Lol Tina. xx

One year later

The pleasure of your company is requested to celebrate the wedding of Valentina Jackson and James Thompson on Saturday 14th February.

Well, what other day could we choose?

Valentine's day chocolates.

More chocolates. Who could resist?

She used to be my best friend. We'd gone through school together, shared teenage secrets, mooned over boys and finally grown into successful, accomplished women. Our jobs took us to different parts of the country but we never lost touch. At least four times a year we met up, and carried on our conversations as if we'd only spoken to each other the day before.

She'd always been beautiful with her shapely figure, sparking blue eyes and long, blonde hair, whereas I was the short, dumpy, nondescript one, but it never occurred to me to be jealous. I was there for her when she needed support after being attacked by her gorgeous, but scum bag, actor boyfriend, or needed a PJs, wine and chocolate girlie night in.

If I so much as looked at a chocolate I put on half a stone, but they were her secret passion, and she could binge eat them without it affecting her modelling career. As she became more well-known, she started to cancel our regular meet-ups, pleading pressure of work as she sunbathed on a millionaire's yacht in the Med, but then she would come running back to me for comfort when it all went wrong.

I plodded along in my respectable managerial job, but at least when she appeared on the front cover of Vogue, I could impress my colleagues with my comment that she was my bestie, and bask in reflected glory.

Mike was charming and good-looking but a bit of a dreamer. He ran a small business and I was assigned to look after his financial requirements, which mainly involved tax returns and claiming allowable expenses. He appreciated my expertise, but I couldn't believe my luck when he asked me out on a date. One thing followed another and we became an item. It was Valentine's day when he took me out for a meal at our local Italian, presented me with a bunch of yellow roses, an engagement ring and told me he was allergic to chocolate.

Naturally, I couldn't resist immediately telling Selena my good news and she responded with a text wishing me every happiness. It was three months before the two most important people in my life met. At first I was delighted they hit it off. What more could I ask than to have Mike as my bridegroom and my best friend as my Maid of Honour?

Six months later I was devastated when he dumped me for Selena. In a way I didn't blame him but she could have any man, why did she take my only love? The papers were full of the hot, top model with her latest squeeze booking the romantic hotel restaurant where they were going to share Valentine's day.

I had arranged the delivery of the box of heart-shaped chocolates to their suite, knowing Mike wouldn't touch them. The message on the card read *"All my love, always. x "*

As I sat alone at home, listening to the clock ticking, I wondered if she would pick her favourite, arsenic-laced one straight away, or save it to savour for later.

When I need you.

There were various versions of this song released in the 1970s, but things aren't always as they seem.

'Take care of yourself, and keep safe.'

'It's only for a few days. I'll be back before you know it. Gotta go, sweetie. Love you.'

The house felt empty without him but at least it would give me a chance to do some spring cleaning, even if it was November. I stripped the beds, even the single ones in the spare room, and bundled the sheets into the washing machine. It was still early so I decided to go the whole hog and take the duvets to the cleaners.

'That's fine, love. They'll be ready by three if you want to pop back then. We close at four.'

'Great. I'll see you later.'

While I was out, I decided to do some food shopping, so the next stop was the supermarket. It felt odd to select ready meals for one, but there was no point in cooking from scratch just for myself. Jack was normally the chef, but using the microwave would save a lot of washing up and give me some extra time.

A quick sandwich for lunch and I was ready to face the next challenge- defrosting the freezer. How on earth did so much stuff accumulate? Expiry date February 2018! All the left-over party nibbles from last Christmas went in the bin, which was soon full to overflowing. I filled two black sacks and felt guilty, knowing some people would have been able to live for weeks on what I had thrown away.

Ice dripped on the kitchen floor as I carried the bags out to the dustbin. Just as well they were collecting tomorrow, and the tiles needed a good scrubbing anyway. The washing machine had finished doing its thing, so time for a quick cuppa before tackling the ironing. While I was having a break, I caught up with a few emails and before I knew it the clock was telling me it was already gone three thirty.

Where had the day gone? A quick dash to collect the duvets, but at that time the traffic was horrendous with all the schools chucking out. The lady in the launderette was turning the closed sign round, but thankfully I left with my fresh, clean bed covers. It was chilly out, and without Jack's warmth in bed I would have been freezing if I'd left it any later, and not retrieved them in time.

The warmth of the house welcomed me as I returned home, double locked the door and went to make the beds. It felt oddly quiet as I wasn't used to being alone in the house. We had both taken this week off to do some decorating and perhaps have a few days away, but Jack's urgent business meeting had changed our plans. Nearly five. It was still too early to phone him. He'd told me they would be going out for a meal after the meeting, so it would be late by the time they returned to the hotel. The battery on my phone was nearly dead, but as I put it on charge a message popped up.

'When I need you, my Darling Jack, you come to me. Don't know how you managed to get

away but three whole days together. Can't wait.
See you very soon. Xxx'

I didn't recognise the number and I trusted Jack, but it seemed too much of a coincidence. If he'd gone to spend time with "her" instead of being on a business trip, had I been deceiving myself we were happy together? But then why had the message come up on my phone, instead of his? Perhaps she was fed up with his promises to leave me and wanted to force the issue. I needed him here, now, so we could discuss our future together, face to face.

With my mind in a whirl I had forgotten the defrosting freezer, my foot slipped on the wet tiles and I blacked out as the floor came up to meet me. It might have been a few seconds, or hours later, I came round to find my leg twisted at a peculiar angle. Stretching to try and pull myself up using the worktop, my limb crumpled under me and I knew no more.

'Where am I? What happened?'

My mouth felt dry as my eyes slowly adjusted to the light.

'Thank God you've come round. It's OK, honey. You're in hospital. I'll get the nurse.'

'Jack? What are you doing here? Why aren't you at your meeting? What's her name?'

Even to my own ears my voice sounded slurred as if I was drunk.

'You've been out for the count for nearly twelve hours. Just take it easy. All those pain killers they've pumped into you are bound to make you feel woozy. Ah, nurse. She's just woken up.'

'Hello there. I'm Mary. How are you feeling? You gave this young man quite a shock. He's been here all night but perhaps you can persuade him to go and have a cup of tea now?'

For the first time I looked at Jack properly. He was a mess. His clothes were wrinkled, his eyes were red-rimmed and he needed a shave.

'What time is it?' I asked.

'Nearly three.'

'In the morning?'

'No, it's afternoon.'

'Jack, go and get something to eat. When you come back, we'll talk. I'm fine now, honestly. Go!'

'OK. I won't be long.'

He looked slightly more human when he returned, and I had managed to unscramble my brain to think more clearly. It seemed he had become worried when I didn't answer his calls or messages, and at first had assumed I'd gone out with friends. By midnight, when there was still no answer he had been concerned, and as his business had finished successfully, decided to come home early. Unlocking the door in the early hours of the morning he had discovered me unconscious on the kitchen floor, and immediately phoned for an ambulance.

'Why did you decide to come home?' I asked. 'And who was the woman?'

'What woman? There were only three stuffy old men but we won the contract. I don't know why, but I had the feeling you needed me.'

'Pass me my phone and I'll show you.'

He had picked up my mobile when he called the ambulance, and I scrolled though his fifteen missed calls before I found the message I was seeking, as well as a later one from the same number.

'Dear whoever you are. I'm so sorry. I realised I had misdialled when Jack turned up and said he'd never received my message saying I needed him. My apologies.'

Seeing the time of the second text, I knew my Jack had been at the hospital with me when I needed him most. Instinct is a weird thing, but sometimes it's as well to trust your sixth sense.

You don't bring me flowers.

Originally written as a short trailer for a TV show, the song tells the story of two lovers trying to hold it together when love has died.

I wasn't impressed the first time I met him. He was with a bunch of cronies in the pub, and they were loud and obnoxious.

'Hey, pretty lady. Why don't you and your friends come and join us? We could do with some female company.'

One of his pals made a grab for me as I passed their table, but I knocked his hand away.

'No thanks,' I replied, 'we can hear you well enough from the other side of the room.'

'No need to get shirty,' he slurred. 'Maybe you need a real man to sort you out.'

The thug stood up to block my way, and I noticed Mark rise from his seat on the far side of the table.

'And maybe you need to learn some manners. I've heard these can be pretty lethal on sensitive parts,' I said, pointing to my stiletto-heeled shoes before pushing past him.

As I joined the group at my own table, I caught Mark's glance and his mouthed 'Sorry.' Shortly afterwards, he helped drag the drunk guy out, and I was able to enjoy the rest of my evening in peace. Although the bar was near where I worked, I didn't go there very often. Usually it was only the Friday after pay day, so I didn't see Mark again for a few weeks. He was sitting in a corner with another man, chatting quietly as they put the world to rights, but he smiled and said Hello as we passed their table.

'Wow. Who's that?' my friend Jane asked. 'He's tasty.'

'One of the guys I was telling you about a few weeks ago,' I replied, for some reason feeling a twinge of jealousy.

A few minutes later a waiter appeared at our table with two drinks, and a note. 'With the compliments of the gentleman over there,' he said, nodding in their direction before moving off.

"We'd be delighted if you would join us, but totally understand if you'd prefer not. This is to ask forgiveness for the unsavoury company from the other week. Best Wishes. Mark."

Reading the note Jane stood up. 'We've got to thank them properly. Come on. I bags the blond one,' leaving me no option but to follow her.

As Mark had dark hair, I assumed she was interested in his friend. That's how it all started. We double-dated for a while until Jane and Paul announced their engagement. Almost out of habit I carried on seeing Mark, although I knew he was not the man for me. He was great company, a good friend, charming, handsome and generous, but somehow the spark was missing. I knew he wanted to take things further, but not wanting to lead him on I stopped answering his calls, and didn't reply to his messages. That was the first time he sent me flowers.

"I'm so sorry if I've upset you. Please forgive me. Let me take you out for dinner on

Friday to apologise. No strings, just friends. Mark. X"

The card was attached to a glorious bouquet of a dozen yellow roses. How could I refuse? We had a lovely meal, and by the time we were on our second bottle of wine, I had the courage to explain exactly how I felt. He accepted my response with a sad face but good grace, and we were able to resume our former platonic friendship. We emailed each other most days, met up for the occasional meal or theatre trip, and became the "plus one" for formal invitations. From then on, every Friday without fail, I received a dozen yellow roses.

It was at Jane and Paul's wedding twelve months later that Mark mentioned he was considering taking up a job offer to work in New York for a year.

'That's great, Mark. I'll miss you but we can still keep in touch.'

'You could always come with me,' he suggested. 'On whatever terms you want. With the salary they're paying me I can easily afford to cover your expenses for a year. We've always got on well and it would be great to have someone I love when I'm surrounded by strangers.'

It was the first time he had said the word "love," although I'd realised long ago how he felt about me.

'It's a lovely idea, Mark, but you know it's not possible. Take the job, have a wonderful time, and when you return, we'll have a celebration dinner so you can tell me all about it.'

He left two weeks later and I assumed my weekly flowers would stop. Not so. Every Friday, regular as clockwork, I received my roses. The months passed and although we still kept in contact, his emails became less frequent. It was nearly a year later I happened to pass the flower shop whose name I recognised from the card, and couldn't resist calling in.

'Good morning. May I help you?' The assistant looked up from wrapping the bouquet of yellow roses on the counter in front of her, with the usual card bearing my name.

'This might sound very odd, but every Friday I receive a bouquet of yellow roses from your shop. I was curious as I know the person who sends them is abroad.'

A smile crossed her face as she replied, 'You must be Donna and the flowers are from Mark? It's so romantic. Did you know yellow roses symbolise friendship and optimism?'

'Yes, I'm Donna, and we're friends, but I wondered how I still receive them when he's away.'

'He arranged it in advance, it must be almost a year ago. Before that he called in personally, and as he was one of our best customers, we promised we'd source and deliver them. Our agreement runs out in a couple of weeks. Is he due back soon? Will you let me know what happens? I love a happy ending.'

Feeling embarrassed I promised I would, and hurriedly left the shop. True to form the flowers arrived the following day, and for the next two

Fridays. Then I received a text message, *"Coming home. Arrive Thursday. Still love you. M. x"*

He did come home but now it's me who buys the flowers. The taxi from the airport was involved in a pile up on the motorway. Every Friday I visit his grave and place a single rose by his tombstone.

The dozen yellow roses I arranged for his funeral bore a card with the simple words:

"You don't bring me flowers any more. R.I.P my friend.'x"

You don't own me.

I loved this song when I was growing up, and was delighted to hear it again recently on a TV advert.

'You're not going out looking like that. For God's sake woman, you look like a tart. It's bad enough you're off gallivanting with your daft friends, leaving me without a dinner on the table. I really don't know why I put up with you.'

'It's not very often. It's Jane's birthday and I haven't seen the girls for ages. There's a pizza leaflet on the kitchen table. Anyway, what's wrong with this dress? You used to like it.'

'It's OK for a girl on the pull, but you're my woman now. What time will you be back?'

'Probably sometime between eleven and midnight. It depends how long we have to wait for cabs. Don't wait up.'

'Oh, so now you're giving me orders. What have I let myself in for?'

'I'm just saying I don't want to disturb you if I get in a bit late. You never tell me what time you're coming home when you go off drinking with your rugby mates. How many times have I cooked a meal, and ended up chucking it in the bin when you roll in drunk and tell me you've already had a curry?'

'Anyone would think I don't pay you with the housekeeping,' Dominic sneered. 'Just go out with your slag mates, but don't coming crying to me if you find yourself up the duff. There's no way I'm paying for someone else's brat. It's not even as if you're any good in bed.'

I'd been so looking forward to this evening but as usual he'd managed to spoil it. It had been six months since I'd caught up with my old workmates, and even then he'd been obnoxious, and insulted people at the firm's Christmas party. Dominic hadn't been like that when we worked together. He'd been good looking, charming and most of the girls in the office fancied him. I'd been flattered when he'd asked me out, wined and dined me, and bombarded me with flowers and loving emails. When he said his landlord had given him notice and he'd nowhere to stay, it seemed the obvious answer to let him move in with me. After all, we'd been lovers for a few months and had seemed totally compatible.

For a while things were great, and it helped to have someone to share the bills, and to have a mutual whinge about our bosses. We worked in different departments so I didn't hear the full story, but the rumours spread like wild-fire around the company, and he was sacked without notice. It made life very difficult for me, as all our colleagues knew we were an item, but he insisted the general manager had it in for him, and it was purely an act of revenge.

At first I believed him, but after several weeks with him lazing around at home, unwashed and making no effort to find another job, he dropped the bombshell on me. He didn't want me working there, listening to their lies, so had told them I was leaving. Even worse, after secretly sending off my CV, he had got me an interview with a new company for the following day. I was fuming at his audacity, but he promised he had my best interests at heart, so when I attended the interview and was offered the job, I took it. Actually, he had done me a favour. The pay was almost double what I had been earning, and there were much better prospects. I was still musing on things when I arrived at the restaurant to be greeted by my old work colleagues.

'Pam. Lovely to see you. I'm so pleased you made it,' Jane said as she gave me a hug. 'All the others are here and you've got some catching up to do. We're already on our second cocktail. What are you having?'

'Hi Pam. How are you? Haven't seen you for ages. We've saved you a place. Come and catch us up with all your gossip.'

'Pam! So pleased you made it. This "Screaming orgasm" is to die for. Try one.'

'I should be so lucky.' Jackie had always been the joker in the pack, but their warm welcome helped to dispel my bad mood, and I found myself relaxing and smiling for the first time in a long while.

'Do you ever hear from "what's his face?" You were well shot of him. Did you get it together with Simon? He was always lusting after you, and when you left, I heard he set up his own company and is going great guns. Give us all the juicy details.'

Sandy's comments brought me back to earth with a bump. It was even more difficult to explain that Simon was now the MD of the company I worked for, and that "What's his face," Dominic, was still living with me. My expression must have given them the answer.

'Don't tell me you're still with that jerk?' Jane asked. 'Sorry, Pam. I don't mean to be rude but you deserve better than that. Right, has everyone decided what they want to eat?'

'Dom by name, and dominating by nature,' Jackie said, then hastily changed the subject when she saw the look on my face.

It was a wonderful evening, and meeting up with the girls gave me the courage to make the decision I'd been putting off. The party split up soon after eleven, with hugs and promises not to leave it so long next time, and I was home by half past.

'Cinderella returns,' Dominic sneered as I opened the door. The place was a mess, beer cans were strewn everywhere, pizzas boxes lay all over the carpet, and it was obvious his slovenly mates had only just left. I gave him an ultimatum; he had a week to pack his bags and leave. That wasn't the best seven days of my life, but when he realised I was serious, he took off without a word of thanks or goodbye.

I hadn't realised how much he had taken over my life, but throwing myself into my work helped ease the loneliness of coming home to an empty house. I didn't see him again until a year later at an awards ceremony for *Business of the Year,* when he accosted me at the prestigious hotel hosting the event. Although he was working there as a waiter, he was drunk and abusive, and I overheard the manager giving him a final warning.

'Hey, Pam,' he slurred. 'What did you do to get an invite here? Sleep your way up? You always liked to make out you owned me, you piece of shit.'

'Actually, I do, Dominic,' I smiled, unable to resist getting my own back. 'Simon and I are now the proud owners of this group of hotels, to go with all our other successful business ventures. That's why we won the award. You don't own me, but I own you. Pick up your cards and have a good life.'

Reviews and contact.

Thank you for reading this book. Now I have a favour to ask. Would you consider leaving a review?
They are helpful to other readers, and invaluable to authors. Even a few words to say you enjoyed it would be greatly appreciated, and only take a minute or two.

More information about the author can be found here:
https://author.to/ValPortelli

www.amazon.com/Voinks/e/B01MVB8WNC.

www.goodreads.com/author/list/16843817.Val_Portelli

If you have any other comments or suggestions, please contact the author via her publishers:
QuirkyUnicornPublications@outlook.com

For advance news of forthcoming publications, the prospect of receiving free copies of the author's books as a member of her review team, and the opportunity to enter prize give-aways, you can sign up for her newsletter here:
https://voinks.wordpress.com/sign-up/

Thank you.